William W. Howland, James Herrick

Historical Sketch of the Ceylon Mission

William W. Howland, James Herrick

Historical Sketch of the Ceylon Mission

ISBN/EAN: 9783337239091

Printed in Europe, USA, Canada, Australia, Japan

Cover: Foto ©Andreas Hilbeck / pixelio.de

More available books at **www.hansebooks.com**

HISTORICAL SKETCH

OF THE

CEYLON MISSION,

BY

REV. WILLIAM W. HOWLAND,

AND OF THE

MADURA AND MADRAS MISSIONS,

BY

REV. JAMES HERRICK.

PUBLISHED BY THE

AMERICAN BOARD OF COMMISSIONERS FOR FOREIGN MISSIONS.

1865.

SKETCH OF THE CEYLON MISSION.

———oo;●;oo———

THE FIELD.

THAT portion of the population of India which speaks the Tamil language numbers about ten millions, occupying the southern part of the peninsula, as far north as Madras, and the northern portion of the Island of Ceylon. The first mission of the American Board among this people was established in 1816, on the island; as the government of Ceylon was at that time friendly to missions, while that of the British East India Company, on the peninsula, was hostile. The southern and central portions of Ceylon are inhabited by the Cingalese — a people of different language and religion. The religion of the Tamil people is Brahminism — the same which now prevails mostly throughout Hindostan; that of the Cingalese is Buddhism. The Tamil inhabitants of the island were originally invaders from the southern part of the peninsula. They dispossessed the other race, and now occupy the northern province, extending down as far as Chilaw on the west and Batticaloa on the east. They number about three hundred thousand, besides a transient population of about one hundred thousand, who have come over within a few years to labor, as coolies, on the coffee plantations in the southern central district.

The mission was established in Jaffna, an island, or rather a cluster of islands, at the northern extremity of Ceylon, separated from each other by narrow creeks, and rising but little above the level of the sea. The district is forty miles long and fifteen broad, containing a population of two hundred and thirteen thousand. Besides the Tamil people, there are five or six hundred Europeans, principally the descendants of the Dutch and Portuguese, who formerly governed the island. There are also a few called Moormen, who are Mohammedans in religion, and are principally engaged in trade. Intercourse is frequent between the Tamil people of the island and those of the peninsula. There being very few large temples on the island, the people often visit those on the peninsula; and the island and peninsula are mutually dependent on each other for various products of the soil.

CHARACTER OF THE PEOPLE.

In estimating the nature of the work to be done by the missionaries among the Tamil people, it is necessary to understand something of their character. It should be borne in mind that the Hindoos, though heathen and idolaters, are not sunk to that depth of degradation found in Africa and the islands of the Pacific. Their dress, their houses, and their manner of life are such as not to require a material change on their becoming Christians. The dress of the higher class is comfortable, neat, and appropriate for the climate, that of the men resembling somewhat the ancient Roman costume. A native, seeing a representation of one of the kings of England, with the flowing robes common in statuary, asked why he was dressed like a Hindoo. Their houses are built in a style fitted to the climate and the habits of the people, and when well built, are comfortable and pleasant. Their principal food is rice, with the fruits, vegetables, and spices of the country. The higher castes are very neat in their habits of cooking and eating, using, it is true, their fingers in eating, but after careful washing; and they are particular never to use the right hand, or *rice* hand, as it is called, for any unclean purpose. Their household and other utensils would, many of them, seem rude to strangers; but they are better fitted for their purposes than they would at first appear to be. The same may be said of their implements of agriculture, and their method of cultivating the soil. In the mechanical arts they show much ingenuity and skill in imitation, but have little power of invention. The architecture of some of their great temples justifies the remark of Bishop Heber, that they " built like giants, and finished their work like jewelers."

LITERATURE.

In striking contrast with those tribes which have not even a written language, their literature is immense. The four Vedas, their most sacred books, when collected, form eleven huge octavo volumes, while the Puranas extend to about two millions of lines. The Ramayana, another of their sacred books, has a hundred thousand lines. Well might Sir William Jones say, " Wherever we direct our attention to Hindoo literature, the notion of infinity presents itself; and sure the longest life would not suffice for a single perusal of works that rise and swell, protuberant like the Himalayas, above the bulkiest compositions of every land beyond the confines of India." In these books there is much truth which deserves admiration, but more that is false and corrupt.

In science as well as in literature, with much that is false and absurd, they have some true principles. They have made considerable progress in mathematics, and have treatises on arithmetic, algebra, geometry, and trigonometry. The ripe scholar and learned Orientalist, Colebrooke, has instituted a comparison between the Hindoo system of algebra and that of the ancient Greeks, and finds reason to conclude that in several most important respects the latter is very far behind the former. In astronomy, many of the elements of their calculations, especially for remote ages, are verified by an astonishing coincidence with the tables of the modern astronomy of Europe, when improved by the latest and most nice deductions from the theory of gravitation. The Brahmins, who annually circulate a kind of almanac, containing astronomical predictions of the more remarkable phenomena in the heavens, — such as the new and full moons, and eclipses of the sun and moon; — are in possession of certain methods of calculation, which, upon examination, are found to involve a very extensive system of astronomical knowledge. But though skilled in the use of the rules contained in his treatise, the Brahmin has no acquaintance with the mode of their structure. In their ideas of geography, chronology, and medicine, there is but little truth, and much that is extravagant, and even ridiculous.

MORAL CONDITION.

It is the *moral* condition of the Hindoos which creates a demand for missionary labor. Though in their habits of life, their employments, their literature, and their science, they are not sunk so low as some other nations, in moral feeling and conduct they are extremely degraded. This moral degradation is the natural result of their religion. Worshiping gods and goddesses into whose history almost no element of virtue enters, who are represented as false to their word, thievish, licentious, ambitious, murderous, — all indeed that is repulsive, malignant, and vile, — it is not surprising that the people should be no better than their deities. Bishop Heber, who was distinguished alike for his learning and accurate observation, and for an amiability of character which led him to view the Hindoos with great charity and kindness of feeling, thus speaks of them : " I really have never met with a race of men whose standard of morality is so low, who feel so little apparent shame on being detected in a falsehood, or so little interest in the sufferings of a neighbor, not being of their own caste or family ; whose ordinary and familiar conversation is so licentious, or, in the wilder and more lawless districts, who shed blood with so little repugnance. The good qualities which there are among them are in no instance, that I am aware of, connected with, or arising out of, their religion ; since it is in no instance to good deeds, or virtuous habits in life, that the future rewards in which they believe are promised. Their bravery, their fidelity to their employers, their temperance, and, wherever they are found, their humanity and gentleness of disposition, appear to arise exclusively from a natural happy temperament, from an honorable pride in their own renown and the renown of their ancestors, and from the goodness of God, who seems unwilling that his image should be entirely effaced, even in the midst of the grossest error."

BONDAGE TO SUPERSTITION.

Connected with their religion there is an almost incredible amount of superstition, which enters into all the details of daily life, and binds them in chains which nothing but divine power can break. They are entangled in its fetters at their very birth, and every day of their life strengthens the bonds, from which they are only delivered by death. At the birth of every child, an astrologer is called to cast its nativity and tell its fortune. While the child is still an unconscious infant, propitious days and omens are constantly consulted for the regulation of all matters of importance in its case ; and as it awakes to consciousness, it awakes to the same hopeless slavery which has bound its parents. If a man is to build a house, the astrologer is consulted as to its position, the exact place for the door, and the exact moment for laying the foundation, which often comes in the night. When the frame is raised, a piece of white cloth, like a flag, is fastened to the ridge, to frighten away birds of ill omen which might light upon it ; and with the same superstition is the building carried on to its completion. The same regard to times and places is had in digging a well, starting on a journey, commencing plowing or harvesting; in short, it enters into almost everything done in the house or in the field. There is also a great attention to signs and omens. If a man, going out of his house to proceed any distance, hears a lizard chirp, or is called by another person, he will return and wait a more favorable moment; so also if he meet near his door one carrying fire, wood, or brown earthen ware. They are in great fear when a child, or one of their cattle, or a garden of vegetables, or anything dear to them, is praised. This will, they suppose, be followed by what is called the blast of the tongue; and if anything is even looked upon with desire, it will be exposed to the blast of the eye, and thus the object of their regard will perish. It is usual, therefore, to place some object in a flourishing garden to divert the attention of the passer-by; and to avoid these and many other evils, and the supposed influence of malignant spirits, they resort to the use of a variety of charms, in which they repose great confidence. The belief in witchcraft, also, is nearly universal. They are much afraid of provoking any one who will be likely to employ the evil spirits against them, and tremble greatly when cursed by any wandering beggar who may not get from them all he asks for. These are only a few of the many superstitions to which they are in cruel bondage.

PREVALENT OPINIONS.

There are certain opinions prevalent among the people which are great obstacles to their conversion to the truth. Among these might be mentioned their ideas of holiness and sin. Their highest conception of holiness is that of their supreme deity, who is represented as without love or hate; above all sense of pleasure or sorrow; in short, destitute of all moral affections. And whoever would be fitted for absorption into this "infinite nothing" must, by a variety of self-inflicted tortures, gradually subdue within himself all feeling and desire. Sin is to break the laws of caste, or to omit some of the numerous rites and ceremonies prescribed by their religion; while to lie, cheat, steal, commit adultery, and wallow like swine in moral pollution, are offenses hardly worth naming. They are only what their gods did before them. All natural evil is the consequence of sin in a previous birth, and must be endured as a penalty. Sin is to be atoned for by works of merit, such as giving water to cows or to travelers, giving rice to Brahmins or to beggars, digging wells or building rest houses for travelers, building and supporting temples.

This idea of justification by works of merit produces among them, as everywhere else, hatred to Christ and the free salvation which he offers. They often say to the missionary, "Preach to us about the one true God; we are willing to hear that; but don't talk to us about Christ." Their ideas of the future life and of fate, their belief that a man is safe in any religion if he is only sincere, and their system of caste, dividing the people into clans hating and scowling defiance at each other, make efforts for their salvation peculiarly discouraging.

Their religion also has a strong hold upon their affections and associations. Their holidays are their religious festivals. Young and old look forward to these days with joyful anticipations. The pomp and splendor, the decorations of the temple and of the car of the idol, the processions and music, the display of fireworks, and the meeting of a multitude, render them occasions of great attraction. To the child, especially, they are the great days, around which pleasant memories cluster long after; and when he meets his companions, they together make a little mimic car, and placing in it an idol of clay, act over the scenes of the festival. Thus is their religion entwined in their affections. It is the religion of their fathers and ancestors, rendered venerable and sacred by its antiquity. Like the lofty towers of one of their own temples, its moss-covered turrets are associated with all the delightsome dreams of childhood, and all the pleasant remembrances of age; and it is not surprising that they consider it heaven-daring sacrilege to attempt to destroy it.

PORTUGUESE AND DUTCH CHRISTIANITY.

The experience which the people of Jaffna had already had of Christianity was not calculated to impress them in its favor. In 1544, Francis Xavier first visited North Ceylon, and baptized from six to seven hundred converts. The Portuguese had already established their power in the southern part of the island, and not long after all Jaffna was brought by them under the power of the church. It was divided into thirty-two parishes, each of which was provided with a chapel and school-house, and, where required, a house for the residence of the Franciscan priest, who was to officiate. The policy of the Jesuits in India was to adopt, almost without qualification, the practices of the idolatry of the country; the old rites and ceremonies, festivals, religious processions, and superstitions; only giving Christian names and titles to the idols which are the objects of worship; and by the aid of government influence, in a few years, almost the entire population of Jaffna, including even the Brahmins themselves, had nominally abjured their religion, and submitted to the ceremony of baptism. There are still some thousands of Romanists in the province, whose worship scarcely differs from that of the heathen, except in the names of the gods and festivals. In moral character they are in some respects lower than their countrymen, especially as they are more addicted to intemperance.

About a century later, the Dutch obtained control of the island. They took possession of the Papal churches in Jaffna, established a school in connection with each, and by a complete union of church and state — making assent to the Helvetic confession of faith necessary to the holding of any office of profit or trust under government — secured a large number of nominal converts. It is represented, that in 1688 the number of Christians in Jaffna amounted to one hundred and eighty thousand. But they were at heart idolaters; and when the English took possession of the island, in 1796, and allowed the natives the free exercise of their own superstitions, the churches were immediately deserted and left to decay, the heathen temples were rebuilt, and almost every vestige of Christianity was soon lost. There is still, now and then, an old man to be found who was baptized by the Dutch, but with no knowledge of Christianity, except, perhaps, an imperfect recollection of the Dutch Catechism.

THE AMERICAN MISSION.

ITS COMMENCEMENT.

The first company of missionaries of the American Board to Ceylon consisted of Messrs. Meigs, Poor, and Richards, with their wives, and Mr. Warren. They arrived in Jaffna during the latter part of 1816. The old Dutch churches, and the houses and premises connected with them, were granted by the government for the use of the mission, and Messrs. Poor and Warren commenced operations at Tillipally, and Messrs. Meigs and Richards at Batticotta. The ruins were rebuilt, and a new system of operations was commenced; not, this time, in reliance upon government influence, or upon any compromise with heathenism, but upon the *truth — the truth as it is in Jesus.* The missionaries sought to bring the Word of God — the Spirit's own weapon — in contact with the hearts of the people, trusting in divine power to make it effectual to their salvation. To hope for success among such a people, with such associations, required a firm faith in the promises of God. Henry Martyn once said, " If ever I see a Hindoo a real believer in Jesus, I shall see something more approaching the resurrection of a dead body than anything I have yet seen." The difficulty of even gaining access to the people for the purpose of bringing them under the influence of the gospel, and the greater difficulty in finding a lodgment for the truth in minds already filled with so much rubbish as were those of the adult heathen, naturally led the missionaries to direct some of their earlier efforts to the children and youth. There was reason to hope that the truth might be sown in their hearts before they were filled with the tares of the adversary, and that, through them, their parents might perhaps be reached. A few teachers of the heathen schools were found willing to enter the employ of the missionaries, and teach Christian lessons in place of the vile stories of heathenism. The parents of the children consented to the change, as they were thereby relieved from the support of their teacher. These heathen teachers would not, of course, feel much interest in teaching the truths of the Bible, nor make much effort to impress them upon the hearts of their pupils. It would not be strange if they should even endeavor to prevent all good impressions; but they were the best that could be obtained at first, and it was considered a great thing to have the Bible taught to heathen children even by teachers really unfit for such a work. The schools were frequently visited by the missionary, and the pupils were called together at the church once every week for religious instruction, besides attending, with their teachers, the services on the Sabbath. A large proportion of their study was Scripture truth, either directly from portions of the Bible, or Catechisms imbodying Scripture history and doctrine. Moreover, the school was a valuable means of access to the people of the village where it was located. It was the place for village meetings — a place in the village where the missionary was on his own ground, and could go and remain through the day, to see those who should call, or for whom he should send, and, if at a distance, where he could make a resting-place for the night. The habits of the people are such that he could come more directly in contact with them there than at their own houses.

VILLAGE SCHOOLS.

These mission village schools are so different from schools in this country that some description of them may be necessary. The building, or school bungalow, as it is called, is a mere roof, raised upon posts, and covered with the fan-like leaves of the palmyra palm, with a floor, raised a foot or more above the ground, made of earth beaten down very hard. Sometimes it is surrounded with a low mud wall, one or two feet high, and at one side there is usually a raised seat of the same material, for the teacher and for the missionary when he visits the school. The children sit, with legs crossed, on narrow mats, spread on the floor. All study aloud, and there is consequently noise, and confusion in proportion to the diligence of the pupils. When the missionary is seen coming, the noise increases. Every boy seems to be trying to drown the voices of all the rest, that he may be heard above them all. This continues till the missionary enters the bungalow, when their books are laid aside, and their attention is directed to him. Nor is it the children alone that are attracted by his approach. The people in the vicinity, and the passers-by, drop in one by one, and sit down. The women steal around on the outside, where they can see and hear, and still be concealed, entirely or in part, by the trees or a hedge. Thus quite an audience is gathered to hear the religious instruction given.

The regular meetings in the villages are usually held in these bungalows in the evening, as the people are industrious, and can not be gathered so easily or in so large numbers in the daytime.

It was considered very desirable to increase the number and efficiency of these schools. After a time some of the teachers became convinced of the truth of what they taught and were apparently subjects of divine grace, and thus better fitted for their work. Many of the schools were supported by missionary associations or Sabbath schools in this country, and thus, undoubtedly, much earnest prayer was secured for particular schools.

EDUCATION OF GIRLS.

The schools were at first composed only of boys. When the missionaries arrived in Jaffna there could hardly be found in the whole district a woman who knew the native alphabet. It was thought quite improper for a female to learn to read. There was to the native mind no conceivable object for it, and it was supposed it would spoil her modesty, endanger her chastity, and render her insubordinate to the other sex. To superintend the affairs of her house, and to minister to the wants of her family, were thought to be not only her first, but her sole duties. It was not till after the mission had been established three or four years, that a few little girls, the daughters or near relatives of the teachers, and a few others whose parents were very poor, could be induced, by the present of a cloth, or some other little reward, to attend the school. When first brought in they could hardly overcome their sense of shame so as to go on with their studies; and those who gave up their daughters for instruction were subjected to no small degree of reproach and ridicule for this

2

departure from national and immemorial custom. Afterward Mr. Poor succeeded in obtaining three or four girls to live upon the premises at Tillipally, and receive instruction. One of them was named Mary Poor, after his excellent mother. After she had learned to read and write, the head-man of the parish came one day to the house to get her signature to a deed transferring some land belonging to the family. The custom is for females to make their mark, or cross, on the deed, when some other person writes the name. When the deed was handed to Mary, instead of making her mark, she wrote, in a fair hand, her name in full. The head-man looked on amazed. He had never seen such a thing before. "Well," said he, "this is good. Now I will send my daughter to school, to learn to read and write." He did so, and others soon followed his example.

RETRENCHMENT — SCHOOLS DISBANDED.

Thus from small beginnings the schools increased and prospered, till, in 1837, there were more than five thousand boys and one thousand girls under Christian instruction in connection with the mission. That year brought a financial crisis in this country, which created a necessity for retrenchment in the missions of the Board. There was no alternative but to disband the schools; and it was done. The views and feelings of the missionaries in reference to the sad necessity thus forced upon them, was thus represented by one of their number: "After my usual lessons with the readers in the schools yesterday, I gave each a portion of the Bible as a present. I told them the reason, exhorted them to read it, not to enter into temptation, and to keep the Sabbath holy — prayed with them, commending them to the Friend of little children, and sent them away — from me, from the Bible class, from the Sabbath school, from the house of prayer — to feed on the mountains of heathenism, with the idols under the green trees; a prey to the roaring lion, to evil demons, and to a people more ignorant than they, even to their blind, deluded and deluding guides; and when I looked after them, as they went out, my heart failed me. O, what an offering to Swamy! — *five thousand children!*" A portion of these schools were afterward gathered again, though they have never, at any time since, amounted to more than two thirds of the previous number.

It is estimated that more than thirty thousand children have, since the commencement of the mission, received instruction in these schools. As the children leave them at an early age, it could hardly be expected that the number of those converted while members of the schools would be large. Still there have been some such cases; and many who have been educated in the seminary and boarding school, and others not educated, who afterward joined the church, received their first impressions while members of these schools. Sometimes cases have come to the knowledge of the missionaries where these children seemed, in a dying hour, to trust in Jesus.

BOARDING SCHOOLS.

Two or three years after the commencement of the mission, a few pupils were gathered into boarding schools at the different stations, where the common branches of Tamil and English were taught, and the more advanced pupils prepared to enter upon a higher course of study. Upon this foundation the Batticotta Seminary for boys was commenced in 1823, and the following year, the Oodooville Female Boarding School for the girls. There was at first a great aversion among the people to allowing their children to eat on the premises of the missionaries; but this was gradually overcome. At Oodooville, two little girls, who had been induced by little presents to come in as day scholars, were prevented from going home one night by a very severe storm. One of them was induced to take food; the other would eat nothing. Some weeks afterward, the father of the girl who had eaten on the premises brought her to Mr. and Mrs. Winslow, and said, "You have been like a father and mother to her, so you may now take her; but tell me what you will do for her. You must find her a husband." They told him that if she continued a good girl, they would take care of her, and he must not come in a few months and take her away. The man had evidently been induced to give up the child by her own entreaties. After this there was less difficulty in inducing others to come, or their parents to give them up. At Batticotta, as the boys were at first unwilling to eat on the mission premises, a cook-house was built for them on an adjoining piece of land which belonged to a heathen, where they were permitted to take their food for more than a year. The establishment was then removed within the mission inclosure, when several boys left the school; but most of them soon returned. Objecting to use the water from wells that had been in common use by the mission families, they decided to clean out a well and reserve it for their own use. As it was during the rainy season, when the springs were full, they found it a harder task than they expected; and they were glad to give up the attempt after one day's hard work, comforting themselves with the conclusion that they had drawn out as much water as there was in the well when they began, and it might, therefore, be considered fit for their use. No further difficulty was experienced from this source, and other prejudices of a similar character were overcome by pursuing a straightforward course for the welfare of the school, without reference to the superstitious notions of the heathen. It has never been the intention of the missionaries to swerve from what they deemed right, out of deference to caste or any other native prejudice.

BATTICOTTA SEMINARY.

The Batticotta Seminary was established for the purpose of raising efficient native laborers, to aid in the work of evangelizing their countrymen. The views of the mission in regard to the school may be understood by the following extract from the prospectus issued at the time of its commencement: "It is the moral influence which the projectors of the present seminary wish to keep primarily and most distinctly in view. Should it even appear singular, they are not ashamed of the singularity of attempting to found a college not so much literary as religious; and indeed literary no further than learning can be made auxiliary to religion. In a word, their design is to teach the knowledge of God, developing all the important relations of the creature to the Creator, for time and eternity." In the second Annual Report, after mentioning the special blessings received in connection with the effusion of the Holy

Spirit at two different times during the year, and that thereby almost every individual had been "aroused to a solemn consideration of those subjects which relate to his present state and future destinies," they said, "We have often prayed, and invited our friends and patrons to unite with us in praying, that God would bless this infant Seminary, that it may be made a blessing. We have labored for the conversion of those instructed in it, that they may become instrumental in converting others. Our hearts are affected by the evidence before us that the Lord has listened to the voice of our united supplications, and crowned our feeble efforts with a larger measure of success than we had dared confidently to expect. By these precious tokens of divine favor we have already received a hundred fold reward, and are greatly encouraged to persevere in our labors."

It was to be expected that a school established from such motives, and under such influences, would be the means of great good. The blessing of God seemed to rest upon it, and its influence was not only seen in the character of the young men thus prepared to labor for the salvation of their benighted countrymen, but in its influence on the whole heathen community; in waking up the native mind, in shaking the confidence of the community in their false systems of science, philosophy, and religion, and in commanding at least a respect for the Bible and its doctrines, the morality it inculcates, and its power to elevate the human mind and character. The whole number of students now living who have been educated in the Seminary is upwards of five hundred. About three hundred and fifty of those who have been connected with it have become members of the church. About one hundred of these are now engaged (1861) directly in mission service, in Ceylon and other parts of India, as native pastors, catechists, teachers, and translators, exerting a great influence in hastening the day of India's salvation. A large number are in government and other employment, where they are exposed to great temptations, but some of them let their light shine in the midst of deep darkness. They have gone as far as Burmah and the Mauritius. One, writing from Pegu to the missionary, stated that he was cut off from all religious privileges, and that his Bible and his closet were his only comfort. Another, who died there, was near the American Baptist missionaries, who testified to his remaining faithful to the end; but others have joined with the heathen, and done much injury.

The Seminary was suspended by the mission in 1855, to prepare the way for a modification of its regulations and course of instruction, so as to secure more directly the object for which it was instituted. There is now (1861) in its place a school called the "Theological and Training Institution," containing about twenty pupils, selected from the most promising candidates for native pastors, catechists, and teachers. Their education is in the vernacular, and free of charge. It is more exclusively biblical than before. Recently there has been a precious revival in the institution, nearly every member having shared in the blessing.

The demand for an English education among the people gave rise, after the suspension of the Seminary, to the establishment of a number of English schools, supported by the people, and taught by natives who had been educated in the Seminary. The most prominent among these is called the "Batticotta High School." It has a Board of five Trustees, two chosen from among the

American missionaries, two native Christians, and the principal. There are from one hundred and thirty to one hundred and fifty pupils, and six teachers, all natives. The principal was formerly a teacher in the Batticotta Seminary, and seems to labor earnestly for the salvation of the pupils. The school is supported by natives, with some assistance received from the Ceylon government. The majority of the pupils are the children of heathen parents; yet it is a Christian school, under very decided Christian influence. This influence, too, seems more natural and healthful, as there is no pecuniary relation to the mission. In the first Biennial Report of the principal is the following statement: " It is a remarkable fact that the more a student shapes his mind for the reception of Bible truths, the more he makes progress in all branches of study." This was lately pronounced, by the government inspector of schools in Ceylon, to be the best school in the whole island, though English missionaries and the government have several flourishing institutions.

OODOOVILLE FEMALE BOARDING SCHOOL.

The Oodooville Female Boarding School was designed to impart a careful Christain education to a select number of female pupils, under circumstances that would seclude them from heathen influences, and be most promising for their moral and intellectual improvement. It was hoped that by this means there would be provided more suitable companions for the young men educated in the mission Seminary. Before this school was commenced, female education had been carried on, to some extent, by the reception of a few girls under the care of the missionary ladies at the different stations; but the superior advantages of a central institution for female pupils being apparent, it was decided to open one at Oodooville, and to receive into it as many of the pupils then under instruction as were willing to go. Twenty-nine were thus received at the outset, in 1824. In 1833 the number had increased to fifty; in 1836 to seventy-five; and in 1837 to one hundred. This is the largest number at one time, and since 1855, when the Batticotta Seminary was suspended, it has been deemed expedient to limit the number of pupils to forty. Nearly three hundred have been educated in the school from its commencement, of whom about four fifths became members of the church, and few have dishonored their profession.* On the other hand, many a church member, weak in the faith, and ready to go back to heathenism, has been reproved and sustained by the wife whom he married from the Oodooville school.

The influence of this institution has been most excellent and far-reaching. The many Christian families scattered over the province, the island, and the continent, exerting a silent but important influence, testify to its usefulness. Many tokens of God's special blessing have been granted, in the frequent revivals which have been enjoyed, and in the uniform prosperity that has attended the institution. There are no results which at the present moment

---

* A table, recently furnished (1865) by Mr. Spaulding, shows that from 1824 to 1864 there were received to the school, from the several mission stations, three hundred and ninety-four pupils. Of these, two hundred and eighty-one have been members of the church, fifty-three have died in good standing, and four under censure ; twenty-two were excommunicated, and there are now in good standing in the church, two hundred and two.

are telling with more power upon the evangelization of the land than those connected with the Oodooville school.

THE PRESS.

For the few first years of the mission, tracts were written upon the leaves of the palmyra, but in 1821, in accordance with the request of the mission for a printer, Mr. J. Garrett arrived with a press. The government of the island being at that time hostile to the operations of the mission, he was peremptorily ordered to leave within six weeks, and the request that he might be allowed to remain longer in a private capacity, on account of the difficulty of leaving during the monsoon, was denied. He accordingly went over to the continent, and the press was taken by the English Church mission. It was thus made available for printing the necessary tracts and books for common use, until 1834, when, the restrictions of government having been removed, the press was transferred to the American mission, and set up at Manepy. It was an occasion of great interest when the first product of their own press was sent around the mission circle, in the form of a small handbill, with the words " *First Fruits* " in English, and the words signifying " *Brotherly Love* " in Tamil. Printing was commenced on a very limited scale; but the importance of this auxiliary so rose in the estimation of the mission, especially in connection with the occupation of the Madura field, that the establishment was greatly enlarged. This continued till 1855, when the press and type were sold to two native Christians, who carry on printing in English and Tamil. During the twenty years in which the press was under the control of the mission, there were printed an average of more than eight millions of pages a year, a large proportion of which were religious tracts and portions of Scripture. Nearly one third of the whole were pages of the Word of God. In 1841 a periodical was commenced, printed semi-monthly, in English and Tamil, which is believed to be the means of much good. It is called " *The Morning Star.*" Since 1855 it has been printed entirely in Tamil. It is taken by heathen subscribers as well as by native Christians. Some years since a child's paper was commenced, called " *The Children's Friend.*"

RESULTS OF MISSIONARY LABOR.

REVIVALS.

In all their labors for the salvation of the people, the missionaries have ever felt that their only dependence for success was upon the influences of God's Spirit. Two or three years after the commencement of the mission, the earnestness of their desires for the outpouring of the Spirit became intense; and they seem to have felt a remarkable assurance that their prayers would be answered. There was also much united prayer among them. The first Monday of the month was spent together, by all the missionaries of the district,

(English Church, Wesleyan, and American missionaries), in prayer and conference. These prayers were answered in the conversion of individuals, and at the commencement of 1824 there was a general revival at all the stations. This was preceded by a day set apart by the missionaries of the district as a season of humiliation, fasting and prayer. During the month of January, interest began to be manifest at several of the stations. At Tillipally, the boys in the school began to inquire what they should do to be saved. In their meetings, every countenance seemed to say, "God is here." At Oodooville, "the Spirit of the Lord seemed to rest on the Sabbath assembly, and many were in tears." At the monthly prayer meeting in February, it is related by one, "The Holy Spirit came down with power, such as probably none of us ever felt or witnessed before, and filled all the house where we were sitting. The brother who first led in prayer in the afternoon, was so much overcome as to be unable to proceed. For some time he had scarcely strength to rise from his knees. The afternoon was spent in prayer, interrupted only by singing, and occasionally reading or repeating a verse from the Bible. It was not *common* prayer, but wrestling with the angel of the covenant, with strong crying and tears." A week or two afterward the awakening extended to Panditeripo, and almost every individual connected with the school there seemed to be "roused at once, and forced to pray, and even cry for mercy." When the missionary, Dr. Scudder, returned from a prayer meeting at Batticotta, late in the evening, he heard, on entering the yard, the boys who were scattered in the garden under the cocoa-nut trees, some alone, and others in little companies, crying, "Come, Holy Spirit," and "God, have mercy." He immediately rang the bell, and they came in with streaming eyes, confessing their guilt and danger. Thus the work went on, extending to all the stations, and everywhere attended with remarkable power, continuing for nearly six months. As the fruit of this revival, between sixty and seventy gave evidence of a change of heart; and early in November of the same year, the Lord granted another refreshing season.

In January of the next year (1825), the fruits of the first revival were gathered into the church. As it was to be a special occasion, arrangements were made to receive them all together, from the different stations. A temporary building was erected for the meeting, in a village central and easy of access to all. The bungalow was one hundred feet long and seventy wide, the top and sides covered with the braided leaves of the cocoa-nut, and lined with white cotton cloth, to give it a light and pleasant aspect. It was erected in a grove of palm trees, in a heathen village which had never before echoed to the songs of Christian worship. Although cholera was raging at the time, there were twelve or fifteen hundred present. It was an occasion of great interest to see forty-one candidates come forward, and profess before the heathen the name of Jesus. Old and young, the gray-haired man of seventy, and the little girl of twelve, stood up together, and, renouncing idolatry, consecrated themselves to the love and service of the one only living and true God. These revivals were types of others, enjoyed at varied intervals, some of them of remarkable power.

NATIVE CHURCH.

There are now (1865) four hundred and seventy-seven members of the native churches. It is an interesting sight to see these Christians, at the occasional gatherings which are held for religious meetings, coming from every part of the field, — Christian parents with their baptized children; Christian young men and women from the schools; Christian teachers with their pupils; catechists, intelligent, earnest laborers in the cause of Christ; native pastors with their flocks, — sitting down together with the missionaries, and celebrating the death of their common Saviour. It is a scene worth crossing the ocean to witness, and must be especially cheering to those who commenced laboring there when all was darkness and the very shadow of death. There is an amount of intelligence among the native Christians unusual in the earlier stages of a mission. A large proportion of them have received a thorough education in the Seminary and boarding school, and are, in this respect, remarkably fitted for training their children, and laying deep the foundations for the Christianity which is to prevail in the land. In some instances, there are already so many of a circle of relatives connected with the church, as to turn the current which has before swept toward the dark gulf of heathenism, and the influence of the family is on the side of Christ; and a large proportion of the family circles in the community have been broken in upon by at least one of their number having become a Christian. These Christian families are scattered here and there in the villages, — lights amid the darkness, witnesses for the true God among the worshipers of devils, — their dwellings *oases* in the desert of heathenism, where the blessing of God descends, where God himself abides. Wherever God's people are, there he is, fulfilling his promises and building up his kingdom; and this fact is a pledge that it shall be established in Ceylon.

Many of those who have been called away by death have remained faithful to the end, and have died in hope of a glorious immortality. In some cases, great joy and triumph over death have been manifested, such as to awaken wonder and admiration even among the heathen around. It is an interesting fact, that many Christians, whose unsteady walk had given their pastors great solicitude, have in the hour of death manifested a steadfast attachment to the Christian faith, and an apparent reliance on Christ, which have encouraged the hope that many of these little ones, even the weak and wayward, will be found at last gathered into the kingdom of God.

CHURCHES WITH NATIVE PASTORS.

Though there were able and faithful men connected with the mission, who held the office of native preachers and of catechists, yet the way did not seem open for ordaining any one as pastor of a native church till 1855. In May of that year, the members of the Batticotta church living on the island of Caradive were organized into a separate church, and Mr. Cornelius, who had labored there faithfully and successfully as a catechist, was ordained as their pastor. The occasion was one of great interest. Caradive is an island containing nearly six thousand inhabitants. When Mr. Cornelius first went there to labor, there was not a Christian in the island, excepting one man, who had been educated in the Seminary, was a suspended member of the church, and has since been excommunicated. Now the missionaries were gathered there to organize a church and ordain the first native pastor. Interest was added to the occasion by the presence of Dr. Anderson, the senior secretary of the American Board, and Dr. Thompson, who accompanied him as a member of the deputation to India. They both took part in the exercises of the occasion, as did also Mr. Meigs, one of the first company of missionaries, and Mr. Spaulding, who joined the mission in 1821. Mr. Cornelius received his education and training on the continent of India, principally in connection with English missionaries. His wife is one of the pupils of the Oodooville school. The Lord has blessed their labors there, and it is hoped they may long be a blessing to the flock under their charge, and to the whole island.

Three others have since been ordained — Thomas P. Hunt at Chavagacherry, David Stickney at Valany, and Francis Asbury at Navaly. Valany is the station of the Native Evangelical Society — an organization of native Christians for the purpose of extending the blessings of the gospel to their countrymen. Mr. Stickney is their missionary; and it is an interesting fact that he is the son of Mary Poor, one of the first among the females who had the courage to break over the bonds of custom, and learn to read and write. She still lives, to see her son a native pastor, and a missionary sent out and supported by her own people.

More recently another church has been organized at Navaly, a village in Manepy; and there are other places where the way seems to be preparing for the formation of churches over whom native pastors may be ordained, and there are promising candidates for the office.

NATIVE MISSIONARY EFFORT.

" Let him that heareth say, Come." It is the first impulse of the soul which has tasted of the water of life to turn to those who are still perishing with thirst, and say, "Come." It was gratifying to the missionaries to see the germ of this instinct of the new-born soul early developing itself in Ceylon, not only in anxiety for near and dear friends, but for all the heathen around. Especially, when laid aside from labor by sickness, was it gratifying to see the natives taking up the missionary work. Mr. Woodward, writing from Calcutta in December, 1821, where he had gone for health and medical advice, says, " When my thoughts recur to Ceylon, I long to be there to witness the salvation of God, with which I believe the people are visited. My heart has been greatly rejoiced to learn, by a letter from Mrs. Woodward, that two girls in our school at Tillipally, who for some time have given evidence of piety, are actively engaged in the blessed work, going from house to house, with the *good news* in their hands, reading to and instructing the poor degraded females, and testifying repentance toward God, and faith toward our Lord Jesus Christ." A few months later the mission mentions, as an interesting fact, " The females who have joined our church seem to take a lively interest in the cause, often seek opportunities, by going to different houses, of communicating truth to their own sex, and are sometimes successful in persuading a few to break away from their former customs, to go to the house of worship, and to listen to a

3

preached gospel." Such efforts were not confined to the females; but in such a country as that, where women are accustomed so to seclude themselves from publicity, and where they are so inaccessible, it was peculiarly encouraging to see Christian females, constrained by the love of Christ, so break over the bonds of custom as to engage in active efforts for the salvation of others. Such voluntary efforts have been continued to the present time, as well by the youth in the schools as by others, and at times with precious results.

In 1832, a society of native Christians, called the Evangelical Society, was formed, for making known the gospel by the support of catechists and teachers, and the distribution of tracts. This society is still in active operation, and is to the Christians of Jaffna what the American Board is to Christians in New England. At first they contributed to the support of one or more catechists, under the direction of the mission; but subsequently they undertook the entire direction of their own agents. The island of Valany, which contains about three thousand inhabitants, was selected as their field of labor, and they were allowed to choose their missionary from any among the men in the employ of the mission who would be willing to be candidates. At that time there was not a native Christian in that island; but the blessing of the Lord seemed to rest upon their labors, and now there is a native church organized, over whom their present missionary, David Stickney, is ordained as pastor. Much interest is manifested by the members of the native churches in sustaining this society, and often much self-denial is exercised by those who contribute for its support. Some give to the amount of one twentieth, one twelfth, and one tenth of their income, and some even more. There, as elsewhere, the poor often deny themselves most to give to the Lord. When a poor girl brings a quart or more of rice, which she has picked up kernel by kernel in the fields, after harvest, it seems a precious gift, and must indeed be precious to Him who sits over against the treasury. The pupils of the boarding school are accustomed to give the value of one meal of food a week, which they voluntarily go without, besides contributing the avails of their earnings by sewing, crochet-work, &c. The contributions to the society now amount to about five hundred dollars a year, or an average of one dollar and twenty-five cents to each church member. The Christians also contribute to other occasional and permanent objects of Christian charity. During the year 1860 they contributed about five hundred dollars as a jubilee offering to the American Board. The members of the churches which have native pastors do what they can toward their support.

The missionary spirit has also been developed by the call for candidates to go abroad, and labor on the islands or on the peninsula. The self-denial necessary for this, especially on the part of a native female, is not readily understood in this country. The difficulties in connection with their domestic system are real and great. They marry very young, generally among their own relatives, and the wife, still a mere child, remains in the house of her mother, or her husband's mother, in a dwelling erected within the yard, or in the adjoining inclosure. If she is sick, her mother, sisters, and cousins are at hand to sympathize with her, to wait upon her, and cook for her family. From others than relatives she would expect neither sympathy nor aid, for in the language of a heathen, who remarked on the care a missionary and his wife had bestowed on a sick native, "The people would as soon tread upon a sick man, who was not a relative, as assist him." This and other circumstances combine to create a very strong feeling in the mind of every native against removing from his or her own little village. If they make the experiment, they seem almost never to think another village tolerable. Each one finds in every other place worse water a hotter sun, and fever more prevalent than in his own. So that when men, and more especially when women, are ready to go abroad to labor for Christ, even upon a neighboring island, it is often as much as for a female in this country to go to foreign lands. The female who leaves America has a long voyage before her; yet other women have traveled for other purposes; but to the female in India, and to all her friends, the thought is a new one, except when women have gone, whole villages in company, to worship at a distant temple. The American female must leave her home and live among strangers; but she knows how to take care of herself, and the step is a common one among her friends. But the Hindoo female, in her own feelings and those of her friends, and to a degree in fact, is an infant, straying out on the wide waste without path, or precedent, or aid. The former is urged on by the plaudits of admiring friends, and often of strangers; but the very mother of the latter will sometimes even threaten sincerely to destroy herself, and the relatives, to work on the holiest, strongest of a daughter's natural feelings, and to express their spite in the most effectual manner, actually withhold needed aid from that mother in distress. Yet there have been those who, in the face of all this opposition, have consented to go abroad to labor for Christ; and though their trials are unknown, and often unappreciated when known, they will be accepted by the Lord of the harvest. The idea of going abroad to labor is becoming more familiar to the native Christians, and there is encouragement to hope that more and more of a missionary spirit will be developed, and more of those who have been educated will be missionaries to their countrymen in various parts of the island, and on the continent.

INFLUENCE UPON THE HEATHEN.

There has as yet been no general turning to the Lord among the heathen in Jaffna. There is no movement even toward a nominal profession of Christianity, as in Southern India. This may arise, in part, from their different circumstances, making the people of Ceylon more independent, and less in need of protection and assistance from foreigners. Any one going to Jaffna from the continent of India, must be struck with the comparatively independent bearing of the natives there. This is probably owing much to the more efficient protection which government has afforded them, and to their position in society as a sort of middle class, there being fewer of the very high and of the low castes. Other circumstances, as the more equal distribution of property, and the abolition of slavery, have probably contributed to the same result. While such characteristics seem in some respects unfavorable, yet, when sanctified, the people will have more Christian enterprise and energy of character, and be better fitted for active service in the work of the Lord.

But, although comparatively very few from among the uneducated heathen have been converted, the result of missionary labor is very apparent in the community. There is now an extensive admission, on the part of the heathen, that Christianity is true, and a good religion, and that it will eventually prevail in the land. It is not uncommon for such old men as are favorably disposed, to say, "Do not urge me to change; I am too old; I must go in the way of my fathers. But here are my children; if they wish, let them become Christians." And some say, "Yes, Christianity will prevail in our children's days." There is also a frequent admission that their own religion is false, though not so common as the admission of the truth of Christianity. They still cling to the idea that their religion will do for them, if they walk according to it faithfully. There is, again, some advance in moral sentiment, especially among those more immediately about the mission stations. Moral character is more highly esteemed. Natives will still lie and steal, when they are tempted to do so; but they are more wary about it, and feel more shame when detected. Heathen parents seem to value the care taken by the mission to protect the morals of pupils in the boarding schools, and approve of the discipline maintained there.

The increased desire for education, especially for female education, is also a result of missionary labor. Whereas, at first, females could hardly be persuaded to attend school, and none came but the children of poor parents, there is now no difficulty in obtaining any desirable number of candidates for admission to the Oodooville school, and they often come from the higher classes. There are, even now, many families of high standing who consider it disreputable for their girls to attend school; but the number of this class is smaller every year. The great eagerness for an English education for boys, indicates a surprising change in the state of the community. This desire for English, on account of the worldly advantage it gives, is undoubtedly excessive; it will prove, in some respects, an injury to the people; and it seems to be a hindrance to other forms of missionary labor. It can not now be controlled, but must in time, like other evils, work its own cure.

Another feature in the community is an increasing disregard of Brahmins and gooroos (or religious teachers), who once received almost divine honors, but now are treated much like other men. The very form which opposition now takes seems to indicate the progress of the influence of truth. The opposers of Christianity no longer look upon it with haughty contempt, as unworthy even of notice; but their learning and talent are brought into requisition to meet it by argument. One of the most noticeable efforts in this direction is the publication of a book of considerable size, which attempts to support the religion of the country by an elaborate argument, going to prove that it is identical with the Mosaic ritual, as recorded in the Bible; and as that was repeatedly declared to be given to be a "statute *forever*," "to all generations," and even Christ and the apostles conformed to it, therefore the Hindoos are right, and Christians are apostates from the true religion.

The state of public feeling is also shown by the fact that when a heathen school was established, a few years since, in opposition to mission schools, because in the latter distinctions of caste were not tolerated, there was influence enough among some of the supporters and teachers of the school, to render it necessary that the Bible should be introduced to make the school successful.

But the most important result of missionary labor among the heathen, and the one which affords the most reason for encouragement, is the general diffusion of the truths of the gospel. Those who are now men and women, forty and fifty years of age, were once pupils in mission schools, read and studied the Bible and Scripture Catechisms, which are not entirely forgotten. The Word of God — "the sword of the Spirit" — is in their minds, ready for the Spirit's work. The way is prepared, as it rarely is among a heathen people, for the establishment of Christ's kingdom. The Lord hasten it in his time.

TRIALS AND DANGERS OF NATIVE CHRISTIANS.

It is difficult for those living in Christian lands to understand the peculiar trials and temptations of Christians among the heathen. Sometimes they are exposed to violent opposition from their heathen relatives. A young man, named Supyan, became interested in the truth early in the history of the mission. He was an intelligent lad of nineteen, whose father was wealthy, and connected with one of the temples near the town of Jaffna; but he allowed his son to attend the school at Tillipally. Having there professed his belief in the Bible, the father was much alarmed, and when he returned home, caused him to be confined, and kept for a time without food. He then ordered him to perform certain heathen ceremonies. Supyan refused, and when shut up in a dark room, made his escape, and fled to Tillipally, where he told Mr. Poor what had befallen him. He took a Testament, and pointing to the tenth chapter of Matthew, from the thirty-fourth to the thirty-ninth verses, said, with tears, " *That very good.*" His father, hearing where he was, sent for him, and as he did not return immediately, came himself, and took him away. They were no sooner out of sight, than his father stripped him of his good cloth, put on him one so poor as to be disgraceful, placed a burden on his head, as though he was a slave, and beat him frequently with a shoe — which is very disgraceful among the Hindoos — until he reached home. Every art was then used to make him renounce Christianity. His relatives said the missionaries had given him some medicine to make him a Christian, and asked what it was. He replied, "The gospel of Jesus Christ." A great variety of drugs were put into his food, to turn him back to idolatry; and an idol feast being made by some of his young friends, he was ordered by his parents to make the customary offering to the idol. When the time came, he entered the little room where the idol was enthroned, pulled off its ornaments, and kneeled down to pray to the true God. One of his companions, looking through the curtain, saw what was done, and told his father, who punished him severely, and sent him for a time to Kandy, in the interior of the island. Afterward his father changed his conduct, and lavished caresses upon him, showed him his various possessions, and told him he should have all if he would give up the idea of becoming a Christian, but if not, he should be an outcast forever. Supyan chose banishment from his father's house, saying, "I do not need house or land if I have an interest in heaven." He attempted to go to Tillipally, but was followed and taken home by force. They then tried to bring him under engagements to marry a heathen girl; but he would not consent, and even tore the contract when offered to him. In short, they put his feet in the stocks, beat him, caused him to be conveyed to the neighboring continent, and at length wearied him out, so that he signed a recantation of Christianity, and ever after seemed settled in heathenism. There have been other cases of similar persecution, though none, perhaps, so severe, or so long continued.

This opposition often comes in just at the time when a person has become interested, and seems on the point of deciding for Christ, and turns him back. Sometimes the mother will threaten to throw herself into the well — a thing not unfrequently done by females in distress. In one case, a son was turned back by the mother throwing herself down in the doorway, and telling the son that if he insisted on going to the church, he should only do it by walking over his own mother. In another case, of a woman among the higher classes, after other forms of persecution failed, the relatives, not willing to give up, and as if in the last struggles of despairing hope, cut down a tree, and prepared the funeral pile to burn the mother alive, in case the woman refused to return to her heathenism, "for *this*," said they, "will atone for the disgrace brought upon us by her becoming a Christian." This had the desired effect. She was overcome, and though dragged unwillingly to the temple at first, afterward went frequently. When exhorted still to trust in Jesus, to take courage, and refuse to yield to temptations, she said, "I know it is my duty. I see that these things are true, and that the customs of the heathen are all folly and against God; but when I feel the blows of my husband, and see the funeral pile of my mother, how can I be bold — how can I trust in Jesus?" She said to Mrs. Spaulding, "If the tree had been cut down to burn *me*, I should not feel it so much; but the thought that my poor old mother must thus suffer for my sake is insupportable." But it is often easier for the native Christians to meet open persecution than to resist the temptations which come in other forms. There is the temptation to yield to their heathen relatives in things which they may consider as of little importance. A heathen mother, perhaps, is going to a festival, and the Christian daughter is tempted to yield to her requests for aid by way of furnishing her with clothing and jewels. A loved and loving mother, a member of the family, observes heathen ceremonies in the house, before the children of Christian parents, and in her love and pity for her grandchildren, will take every opportunity she can to rub upon their foreheads the sacred ashes, or prejudice their minds in favor of her gods; and the parents can not easily prevent it, without casting out their own mother from house and home. A child is perhaps sick: the grandmother and other relatives, after the failure of other means, urge the resort to some charm, or to call some celebrated heathen doctor, who gives medicine with incantations; and in the distress and anxiety of the mother, she yields. She herself has been educated, from her earliest infancy, to have confidence in such things, and it is difficult to free her mind from the influence of such education. She will almost involuntarily start as the lizard chirps, or some other unfavorable omen suddenly surprises her; and when sickness or death comes into the family, and loved friends attribute it to the neglect of the gods, it needs a firm faith to stand unfaltering till the storm has blown past. Again, there is a wedding in the family, conducted, of course, with heathen ceremonies. The Christian brother or sister must either be present, and thus give sanction indirectly to idolatry, or be cut off from all sympathy with family friends. A neighbor comes in on the Sabbath, knowing it to be a day of leisure with the Christian, to avail himself of his superior education, to get some writing done, a deed or a petition drawn, and it is hard to refuse. For purposes of irrigation, it is usual for several neighbors to own a well together; and as it takes three persons to draw water for watering the fields, they assist one another. When one is a Christian, the others will refuse to assist him at all, if he will not help them on the Sabbath. In like manner they are dependent on one another for bullocks in plowing, and assistance in harvest; and the heathen are on the watch to catch the Christian in matters of his religion, and are sure to make demands which will interfere with it.

The most common device is to entangle a young Christian in a heathen marriage. The heathen father of a Christian young man will perhaps pledge to another man, under a severe penalty, which can not be incurred without great loss and sacrifice, that his son shall marry the man's daughter; and the son, in love and pity for his father, is tempted to yield, flattering himself with the usually vain hope that he can succeed in making his wife a Christian. A very frequent temptation to a heathen marriage is the large dowry which many of the heathen are now willing to offer with their daughters, to an educated young man, who is consequently called to choose between a Christian wife with little or no dowry, and poor relatives, and a heathen wife with a large dowry, and connected with a wealthy family. He has seen neither of them, and can not till he is married. The relatives of both are heathen, and in that country a man weds, with his wife, the whole circle of relatives. The temptation is strong — the most common and the most successful. Not a few have fallen into this pit, and have been lost, at least for a time. Some have returned, and a few have brought their wives with them.

To meet these trials of their faith, the native Christians have little strength of moral character. Born of heathen parents; inheriting the debasing influence of heathenism, which has been accumulating and concentrating for so many generations; educated in an atmosphere of idolatry and sin, where truth is literally fallen and trampled upon in the streets, — where lying, stealing, and adultery are no disgrace; it is no light thing for them to "stand up for Jesus" at all times and under all circumstances.

Again: if Christians in this land, with all the overwhelming evidence they have of the truth of their religion, do sometimes have the doubt come into their minds for a moment, whether it is true, after all, much more may those where the whole community, comprising the wealth and talent of the land, is against them, whose religion boasts of an antiquity which runs back for ages beyond the Mosaic history, and who affect to despise the few foreigners who have come in, and are attempting to introduce a new religion of so recent a date, and which has nothing grand or imposing connected with its history or its worship. It is not surprising that faith sometimes falters. One of the missionaries, after giving the native Christians an account of the confirmation of Scripture by the discoveries in Nineveh, remarked that to them these things were not of so much importance in confirming Scripture, as they did not need them. A native preacher immediately replied, " To us these things are like eyes to the blind." Similar were the remarks made concerning a wandering Jew, who came along a few years ago. They had never seen a Jew before, and as they heard him chant the Hebrew Scriptures, they seemed to have a new realization of the truth of the Bible. Here was one of the very people whose history occupies so prominent a place in its pages.

And when these Christians do yield to their doubts and temptations, and fall away, it is a more serious matter than an apostasy in this country. The miracle of a renewed heart acting upon the life, is the standing miracle which testifies to the truth of Christianity before the world ; and he who professes to have been renewed needs to be very free from faults to have any influence in favor of the truth. The position of the catechists and native pastors is often very trying, on account of the little confidence the people have in their sincerity. A heathen will sometimes say to them, " Yes, I will listen to what you have to say as a personal favor to *you*. It is your work to talk to us, for which you are paid. It is therefore my duty, as your friend, to listen to you, to encourage you in your business."

These Christians should therefore be sustained and strengthened by the prayers of those more favored and less tempted in this land. Let them be especially remembered in the monthly concert; let them not be forgotten in the church prayer meeting ; and let them at least be remembered by one petition in the daily family and private devotions of Christians.

A word may properly be said here, also, respecting the need of prayer for the children in schools.

The Hindoos have a proverb, " The father and mother are the first god the child knows." There is an important truth in this saying. The Creator evidently designed that the child should follow the steps of its parents, and be by them trained in piety and righteousness. It is an unnatural state of things when a child has parents unfitted for this work, and must be taught by others that they are wrong, and that he should forsake their instruction and their ways. These children are objects of compassion and sympathy. The missionaries tell them one thing, and their own beloved father and mother the reverse. Which will they naturally believe ? With the child, also, the wonderful miracles said to be performed by the heathen gods have much influence. The miracles of the Bible are stories of past ages. Their own sacred books have not only more wonderful stories of the past, but their religion boasts of its present miracles. The child is really perplexed. A little girl in Manepy, who was told that one of their gods, at a temple a few miles distant, caused men's tongues, which had been cut off, to grow out again, went away, and prayed, " O God, if the god which makes the tongue grow is God, tell me; if Jesus Christ is God, tell me."

CONCLUSION.

The way seems to be remarkably prepared in Jaffna for an outpouring of the Spirit upon the whole community. The thirty thousand who have studied the Bible in the village schools are scattered all through the land. What an encouragement for Christians to pray that God will bless his own Word! Revivals heretofore have been confined principally to the boarding schools; but there seems reason to hope for an awakening among the masses. This is the great want of the mission. It has come to a point in its history where it seems as though it could hardly continue without it.

Much labor has been bestowed, for many years, and much prayer has been offered by the faithful laborers. Some of those who have gone forth weeping, bearing precious seed, have gone to their reward. Their sacred dust consecrates the soil on which they labored. Their names will not soon be forgotten in Jaffna. Others are still spared — may it not be hoped to rejoice over a rich and abundant harvest? But this blessing depends much upon the prayers of Christians in the United States. In former revivals in Ceylon, the missionaries used to say they knew when Christians were praying at home before the news came by mail.

The following persons have been connected with the Ceylon mission : —

	Joined the Mission.	Left.	Died.
Rev. James Richards, ...	1816		1822
Mrs. Sarah Richards, ...	1816	1823	
Rev. Edward Warren, ...	1816		1818
Rev. Benjamin C. Meigs, ...	1816	1858	1862
Mrs. Sarah M. Meigs, ...	1816	1840	
Rev. Daniel Poor, ...	1816		1855
Mrs. Susan Poor, ...	1816		1821
Mrs. Ann K. Poor, ...	1823	1855	
Rev. Miron Winslow,*	1819		1864
Mrs. Harriet W. Winslow, ...	1819		1833
Rev. John Scudder, M. D.,*	1819		1855
Mrs. Harriet Scudder, ...	1819		1849
Rev. Levi Spaulding, ...	1819		
Mrs. Mary C. Spaulding, ...	1819		
Rev. Henry Woodward, ...	1820		1834
Mrs. Lydia Woodward, ...	1820		1825
Mrs. Clarissa Woodward, ...	1826	1836	
Rev. Geo. H. Apthorpe, ...	1833		1844
Mrs. Mary R. Apthorpe, ...	1833		1849
Rev. Henry R. Hoisington, ...	1833	1850	
Mrs. Nancy L. Hoisington, ...	1833	1850	
Rev. Samuel Hutchings, ...	1833	1842	
Mrs. Elizabeth C. Hutchings, ...	1833	1843	
Rev. James R. Eckard, ...	1834	1843	
Mrs. Margaret E. Eckard, ...	1834	1843	
Nathan Ward, M. D.,†	1833	1847	

* Removed to Madras, 1836.

† Mr. and Mrs. Ward sailed again, to rejoin the mission, in 1860. Mr. Ward died on the passage. Mrs. Ward left for the United States in 1865.

4

	Joined the Mission.	Left.	Died.
Mrs. Hannah W. Ward, ...	1833		
Mr. Eastman S. Minor, ...	1834	1851	
Mrs. Lucy B. Minor, ...	1834		1837
Mrs. Judith M. Minor, ...	1839	1851	
Rev. John M. S. Perry, ...	1835		1837
Mrs. Harriet J. Perry, ...	1835		1837
Miss Eliza Agnew, ...	1839		
Miss Sarah F. Brown, ...	1839	1841	
Rev. Edward Cope, ...	1840	1848	
Mrs. Emily K. Cope, ...	1840	1848	
Rev. S. G. Whittelsey, ...	1842		1847
Mrs. Anna C. Whittelsey, ...	1842	1848	
Rev. Robert Wyman, ...	1842		1845
Mrs. Martha Wyman, ...	1842	1845	
Rev. John C. Smith, ...	1842		
Mrs. Eunice P. Smith, ...	1842		1842
Mrs. Mary Smith, ...	1843		
Rev. Adin H. Fletcher, ...	1846	1850	
Mrs. Elizabeth W. Fletcher, ...	1846	1850	
Rev. Wm. W. Howland, ...	1846		
Mrs. Susan R. Howland, ...	1846		
Rev. W. W. Scudder,*	1846	1852	
Mrs. Catharine E. Scudder, ...	1846		1849
Rev. Eurotus P. Hastings, ...	1846		
Mrs. Anna Hastings, ...	1853		
Samuel F. Green, M. D., ...	1846		
Mrs. Margaretta W. Green, ...	1852		
Rev. Joseph T. Noyes,†	1849	1852	
Mrs. Elizabeth A. Noyes,†	1849	1852	
Rev. Cyrus T. Mills, ...	1849	1853	
Mrs. Susan L. Mills, ...	1849	1853	
Mr. Thomas S. Burnell,†	1849	1855	
Mrs. Martha Burnell,†	1849	1855	
Rev. Marshall D. Sanders, ...	1852		
Mrs. Georgiana K. Sanders, ...	1852		
Rev. Nathan L. Lord,†	1853	1860	
Mrs. Laura M. Lord,†	1853	1860	
Rev. Milan H. Hitchcock, ...	1858	1860	
Mrs. Lucy A. Hitchcock, ...	1858	1860	
Rev. James Quick, ...	1858		
Mrs. Maria E. Quick, ...	1858		
Rev. James A. Bates, ...	1861	1864	
Mrs. Sarah A. Bates, ...	1861	1864	

* Transferred to Arcot.   † Transferred to Madura.

SKETCH OF THE MADURA MISSION.

———∞⦂⦂∞———

THE FIELD.

THE field of the Madura mission is the Madura Collectorate, in Southern India. It lies between the ninth and eleventh parallels of north latitude, and between the Gulf of Manaar on the east and the district of Travancore on the west. It has a surface of ten thousand square miles, and a population of nearly two millions.

The face of the country in the eastern part is level. In the western part, mountains are often found rising abruptly from level plains. A range, seven thousand feet in height, extends along nearly the whole of the western border, adding much not only to the beauty of the scenery, but to the fertility and healthfulness of the district.

SOIL AND PRODUCTIONS — CLIMATE.

The soil is generally rich, and when rain falls plentifully, in its season, is highly productive. The most valuable productions are cotton, castor-beans, tobacco, rice, and several kinds of grain and pulse unknown in this country. Many varieties of tropical fruits are found, of which the most abundant are cocoa-nuts, tamarinds, and plantains.

The climate is hot and dry. For many successive days, in the hot season, the thermometer in the house ranges from 96° to 100° in the afternoon, and the nights are but little cooler. In the coolest part of the year, the thermometer in the open air never indicates a lower degree of temperature than 69° or 70°.

The climate is, however, free from great and sudden changes, and comparatively healthy. For twenty years previous to 1865, during which time there have been, on an average, from fifteen to twenty adults in the mission, only two have died there, (besides one who was drowned,) and one of these was an invalid before leaving America.

Of the present and former missionaries, nearly twenty, including persons of both sexes, have spent from fifteen to twenty years in the mission, without leaving it.

The health of the mission is greatly promoted by the Sanitarium on the Pulney Mountains, in the Madura district. The location is about seven thousand feet above the plains, and the air is cool and bracing. In the cool season, the climate is much like that of New England in the clear days of October. Even in the hottest part of the year, when, upon the plains, the lightest garments are burdensome, thick clothing and a little fire are needed for comfort. No one who has not experienced the heat of India, can imagine how much a person is refreshed by a change, for a little time, from the burning plains to the top of these mountains, and how great reason the members of the Madura mission, and other foreigners in that part of India, have to be grateful for the delightful retreat afforded by them.

THE PEOPLE — TEMPLES AND FESTIVALS.

The great mass of the people in this district are heathen, though Mohammedans are numerous in the large towns, and there are many Roman Catholics. All speak the Tamil language, and several, who came originally from regions further north, also speak Teluga.

There are many ancient temples in the Madura district, which have been much resorted to by one generation after another, for hundreds of years. Several of these are large, and were built at enormous expense. The largest and most celebrated is the temple in the city of Madura, devoted to Minachy, the tutelar goddess of that place. She is supposed to be the deified daughter of one of the Pandian kings, by whom this part of India was ruled for several centuries, both before and after the commencement of the Christian era. This temple was begun by one of the earlier kings, and enlarged and beautified by his successors, who expended vast sums of money upon it, and gave lands of great value for its support. It covers several acres of ground, and has four high pagodas, or towers. Two or three elephants are always kept in it, which are used in processions on great occasions. Four or five images of horses and bullocks, made of wood, and covered with plates of gold and silver, belong to the temple, upon which the image of the goddess is sometimes placed, and carried through the streets of the city.

A large number of "dancing girls" are connected with this temple, who were devoted to it by their parents, or born of those previously thus devoted. A part of their duty is to sing and dance in the temple. They are as corrupt in character as many of the women in Corinth were in the days of the apostle Paul. Several men are also connected with it, who play upon drums, and other instruments, the sound of which may be heard all over the city, every morning, before the dawn of day.

In passing the wide gates of the temple at night, one is astonished at the number of lamps kept burning. They are so arranged as to present a very striking appearance, the object of them being to make a show rather than to give light. An annual festival is observed in honor of this goddess, attended by thousands of people from all parts of Southern India, and from the island of Ceylon.

There are many choultries, or rest-houses, in and around Madura, built for the accommodation of people who attend this festival. One within the walls of the temple is called "the thousand pillared choultry," from the number of stone pillars by which the roof is supported. During this festival, the image of the goddess is brought out, covered with ornaments of precious stones set in gold, placed upon a large and highly decorated car, and drawn round the city, attended by the beating of drums, the blowing of horns, and the shouts of the great multitude.

The last thing that takes place, from year to year, is the marriage of Minachy to Sokalingam, another name of Siva. Alagar, the beautiful one, a name given to Vishnu, is annually brought down from his temple at the foot of Alagar Mountain, twelve miles from Madura, to take part in the marriage ceremony. Ilis temple is large and richly endowed.

The following temples also are much celebrated : One devoted to Suprimanian, at Secunder Molie, four miles from Madura, at which there is a monthly as well as an annual festival; another devoted to the same deity at Pulney; and one for the worship of Siva, on the island of Ramesuram, near the eastern coast. Pilgrims resort to this temple in great numbers, on account of the supposed efficacy of the water there in cleansing from moral pollution.

ORIGIN AND MEMBERS OF THE MISSION.

Rev. Levi Spaulding, of the American mission in Ceylon, visited the continent in January, 1834, and selected Madura as the site of a new mission among the Tamil people.

In July, 1834, Messrs. Hoisington and Todd, of the Ceylon mission, made a visit to Madura. Mr. Hoisington returned after two months, and Mr. Todd remained. He buried his wife in September, 1835, and subsequently married Mrs. Woodard, who died in June, 1837. His own health failed, and he left for America in January, 1839.

Rev. Daniel Poor, who had labored in Ceylon nearly twenty years, visited Madura in October, 1835, and removed there with his family the following March. He remained in this mission, laboring with great earnestness, till July, 1841, when he returned to Ceylon. His name is still remembered with great respect among the natives in Madura. Rev. Messrs. A. C. Hall and J. J. Lawrence arrived in Madura with Mr. Poor. " This reënforcement," it is said, " together with the preaching of Mr. Poor, and the books brought by him, excited great attention among the natives."

The names of those who are or have been members of this mission, with the year of their arrival in the field, and the year of the leaving or death of those who are no longer members, are presented in the following table. Of those who left early, Messrs. Echard and Poor, with their wives, returned to Ceylon, where they were laboring before going to Madura. Mr. and Mrs. Cope also joined the Ceylon mission, and Mr. and Mrs. Ward, and also Mrs. Dwight, (as Mrs. Winslow,) went to Madras.

	Joined the Mission.	Left.	Died.
Rev. Wm. Todd, ...	1834	1839	
Mrs. L. B. Todd, ...	1834		1835
Mrs. C. E. Todd, ...	1836		1837
Rev. James R. Eckard, ...	1835	1836	
Mrs. M. E. Eckard, ...	1835	1836	
Rev. Alanson C. Hall, ...	1835	1836	
Mrs. Frances A. Hall, ...	1835		1836
Rev. J. J. Lawrence, ...	1835		1846
Mrs. M. H. Lawrence, ...	1835	1847	
Rev. Daniel Poor, ...	1836	1841	
Mrs. A. K. Poor, ...	1836	1841	

	Joined the Mission.	Left.	Died.
Rev. Robert O. Dwight,	1836		1844
Mrs. M. B. Dwight,	1836	1845	
Rev. Henry Cherry,	1837	1849	
Mrs. C. H. Cherry,	1837		1837
Mrs. Jane E. Cherry,	1839		1844
Mrs. Henrietta Cherry,	1844	1849	
Rev. Edward Cope,	1837	1839	
Mrs. E. K. Cope,	1837	1839	
Rev. Nathaniel M. Crane,	1837	1844	
Mrs. Julia A. J. Crane,	1837	1844	
Rev. C. F. Muzzy,	1837	1857	
Mrs. S. B. Muzzy,	1837		1846
Mrs. M. A. Muzzy,	1848	1857	
Rev. Wm. Tracy,	1837		
Mrs. E. F. Tracy,	1837		
Rev. F. D. W. Ward,	1837	1843	
Mrs. Jane S. Ward,	1837	1843	
John Steele, M. D.,	1837		1842
Mrs. Mary S. Steele,	1837	1843	
Alfred North,	1843	1847	
Mrs. North,	1843		1844
Rev. H. S. Taylor,	1844		
Mrs. M. E. Taylor,	1844		
Rev. James Herrick,	1846		
Mrs. E. H. Herrick,	1846		
Rev. John Rendall,	1846		
Mrs. J. B. Rendall,	1846		
Rev. Edward Webb,	1846	1864	
Mrs. Nancy A. Webb,	1846	1864	
Rev. George W. McMillan,	1846	1854	
Mrs. R. N. McMillan,	1846	1854	
Rev. John E. Chandler,	1847		
Mrs. C. H. Chandler,	1847		
Rev. George Ford,	1847	1853	
Mrs. Ann J. Ford,	1847	1853	
Rev. Charles Little,	1848	1858	
Mrs. Amelia M. Little,	1848		1848
Mrs. Susan R. Little,	1854	1858	
C. S. Shelton, M. D.,	1849	1855	
Mrs. H. M. Shelton,	1849	1855	
Rev. J. T. Noyes,	1853		
Mrs. E. A. Noyes,	1853		
Rev. T. S. Burnell,	1855		
Mrs. Martha Burnell,	1855		
Rev. W. B. Capron,	1857		
Mrs. S. B. Capron,	1857		
Rev. Charles T. White,	1857		
Mrs. Anna M. White,	1857		
Rev. Edward Chester,	1859		
Mrs. Sophia Chester,	1859		
Miss Sarah W. Ashley,	1859	1864	
Rev. George T. Washburn,	1860		
Mrs. Eliza E. Washburn,	1860		
Rev. David C. Scudder,	1861		1862
Mrs. Harriet L. Scudder,	1861	1863	
Rev. Nathan L. Lord, M. D.,	1863		
Mrs. Laura W. Lord,	1863		

Rev. J. Scudder, M. D., labored two years in this field, from April, 1847, without becoming a member of the mission.

Previous to the establishment of the American mission in Madura, no Protestant missionary had ever resided in the district. Subsequently, the "Gospel Propagation Society" supported two or three missionaries, with a few catechists and schoolmasters, in the district, for several years. But in 1859 the agents of this society were withdrawn ; and by a mutual agreement, the whole of the Madura district, except a part of Ramnad, was committed to the American mission.

The whole number of ordained missionaries, who have been connected with the mission, is twenty-eight, four of whom united with other missions on leaving this. The mission has been in existence thirty-one years, and the average number of its resident members has been between eight and nine. It has enjoyed the services of a mission physician just half the time from its commencement. Leaving out of the account those who joined other missions on going from this, the average time thus far spent in actual service, by the present and former members, has been ten and a half years.

MISSIONARY OPERATIONS AND THEIR RESULTS — EDUCATION.

1. *Tamil Free Schools and English Schools for the Heathen.*

During the early years of the mission, great importance was attached to education as a means of evangelizing the people. Free schools for heathen children, and taught by heathen masters, were for a time supported in large numbers. Two were established at once, and several more the following year. In two years from the commencement of the mission, there were thirty-five schools, and the next year sixty, containing twenty-two hundred and eighty-four pupils. In 1840 the number had increased to ninety-nine, and in 1844 there were one hundred and fourteen schools, containing thirty-three hundred and fifty-three pupils, of whom one hundred and fifteen were girls. There were also four called select schools, containing one hundred and fourteen pupils, somewhat more advanced than those in the free schools generally. This was the largest number of free schools for heathen children supported at any one time. They began to decline soon after, and five years later there were only thirteen. In 1850 there were ten, six of which were taught by Christian teachers. Four years later there were no schools exclusively for heathen children, and since that time none have been employed as teachers, who were not, nominally at least, Christians. In the mean time several schools had sprung up, most of them more remote from the station centres, different in character, and established for a different purpose. These will be spoken of hereafter.

What has been the result of the labor and expense bestowed upon the system of education described above can not be definitely told. There can be no doubt that those schools served, to some extent, to conciliate the people, and that a vast number of children learned to read who would not have learned without them, is certain. It is also certain that the teachers generally, thousands of their pupils, and many other persons, gained considerable knowledge of the principles of Christianity by means of the schools. Lessons were regularly learned from the Bible and Catechisms, both by teachers and pupils, and recited to the superintending missionary. In the Annual Report for 1841 it was said, "About a thousand of the pupils in the native free schools are able to read, and nearly the whole number" (upward of three thousand,) "have committed to memory the ten commandments, the Lord's Prayer, and a small Catechism." Teachers and pupils were required to attend meetings on the Sabbath. Each school was frequently visited by the missionary as well as by catechists, and made a place of preaching and giving religious instruction; yet very few of the teachers or pupils have thus far become Christians, and many of them have died without leaving any evidence that they were benefited, spiritually, by the truths made known to them. Many of these remarks apply equally to English schools, two of which were early established, and one continued for twenty years.

2. *Station and Village Schools.*

At each station under the care of a resident missionary, there is a vernacular school, taught by a Christian, and generally superintended by the missionary's wife. All other free schools are in village congregations, having been established with direct reference to the children of people who have embraced Christianity. Heathen children, however, are usually allowed and encouraged to attend. The teachers are all Christians, and the same lessons are taught to both Christian and heathen children. The number of station and village schools, at the end of 1864, was sixty-four, and of pupils in them, eleven hundred and eighty-six.

It is the aim of the mission to secure the attendance of all Christian children of proper age; but such is the poverty of many of the parents, and their inability to appreciate the worth of education, that they cannot be induced to send children regularly to school who are able to work.

3. *Boarding Schools.*

Within five years of the origin of the mission, six boarding schools were established; four for boys and two for girls. One of the latter was supported for a short time by individuals in the country. Those for boys were established chiefly for the purpose of furnishing the mission with well-educated native assistants, while a secondary object was the general diffusion of Christian knowledge. The object of the schools for girls was twofold — to promote female education, and to furnish suitable companions for catechists and teachers. These schools were at first all open to heathen children, but were taught by Christian teachers. For several years the English language was taught in them all, and pupils were received before even learning to read in their own language; but rules were at length adopted requiring at least an ability to read the vernacular, as a condition of being received to a boarding school. At a later period, heathen children, and children from without the Madura district, were excluded. The study of English was early dropped in the female boarding schools, and afterward in the schools for boys.

The boys' boarding schools have all been discontinued. One reason for this was their expense; another, the impression that, by drawing from the village schools the sons of catechists, teachers, and others of the more promising boys, their influence was prejudicial to those schools; and the hope was entertained that the seminary, in connection with the village schools, would be able to meet the demand for the education of native assistants. Many pupils were hopefully converted while in the boarding schools, and others after going from them to the seminary.

In 1846, the two female boarding schools were united in the school at Madura, which has been prosperous and very useful until the present time. The average number of pupils for the past ten years has been forty-six. All were nominally Christians when admitted, and many have since been received to the church. Many of the graduates are wives of native pastors, catechists, and teachers, and several have been themselves employed as teachers.

4. *The Seminary.*

The mission at first relied principally upon the Batticotta Seminary, in Ceylon, to furnish the native assistants needed; but it was found that the requisite number could not be obtained from that source. It was thought, too, that those who came from there were less useful than if they had been born and educated upon the continent. A representation was made to the Prudential Committee, and leave was obtained to establish an institution within the mission for the express purpose of supplying it with native helpers.

In September, 1842, a seminary was opened at Tirumangalam, by Mr. Tracy as principal, with thirty-four students, all received from the four boarding schools. Ten were members of the church. At first, the seminary, like the boarding schools, was open to the heathen and Roman Catholics as well as to Protestant Christians. Some were received from places without the limits of the mission, and several, who were heathen or Catholics when they entered, *were afterward converted.*

For several years the English language held a prominent place in this institution, as in the boarding schools, and all the pupils spent much of their time in this study. There was then a great scarcity of books in the Tamil, suitable to be used as text books, or to be consulted for general knowledge and improvement. There was also then, as now, a great desire on the part of the natives to learn English.

In 1845 the seminary was removed from Tirumangalam to Pasumalie, the requisite buildings having been erected. The location at Tirumangalam was in some respects unfavorable, and there were not suitable buildings there. The present location is in all respects a desirable one.

The year 1847 was an important one to the Madura mission, on account of the action then taken upon the subject of caste, which had a special influence upon the seminary. The case is thus stated, in a report of the mission relative to the seminary, in 1855: "The year 1847 formed an era in the history of this institution. The mission took action on the subject of caste in July, having direct reference to the catechists and church members; and it was the occasion of some excitement in the seminary, from the fact that many of the catechists, and others affected by the caste movement, had sons in the institution at the time. The object of the seminary being to raise up helpers for the mission, it seemed inconsistent to admit, or even to retain in the institution, those who, by observing the rules of caste, would be unqualified to enter the service of the mission as catechists, after having completed their course of study. In consequence of the action of the mission in October, 1847, the seminary was nearly disbanded, only one of the teachers and nine of the students having complied with the requisition of the mission. Some of the scholars, and one of the teachers, afterward returned. A few months later, a class of twelve, mostly Christians from our own district, and of low caste, were received." Since that time very few students have been received from abroad, and nearly all have come from Christian families.

In 1849 the course of study was so modified as to diminish the study of English, except in the case of a comparatively small number of the most promising students. Three years later a class was received, consisting of fifteen young men from the different stations, who had been instructed, more or less privately, by catechists and missionaries. They knew nothing of English, studied only Tamil in the seminary, and left the institution after two years, and engaged in mission service. From that time onward, a similar class has generally been connected with the institution.

The English language received less and less attention, until, in 1859, it was discontinued as a regular study. The missionaries have generally regarded this as an important change. One strong reason formerly existing for the study of English has been removed by the great increase, in later years, of good books in the vernacular. The expense of education is thus diminished, while young men, having a knowledge of their own tongue alone, are subject to fewer temptations than those understanding English, and are retained in mission service on lower pay.

In 1857, two catechists, previously accepted by the mission as candidates for the pastoral office, were sent to the seminary for a year, that they might become better fitted for their future duties. They made good improvement, and were afterward ordained. Since then there have usually been a few catechists engaged in study at the seminary, some to increase their qualifications for the work of catechists, and some to fit themselves for pastors. Most have highly appreciated the advantages enjoyed there, and have been much benefited by them.

The principal of the seminary has occupied the place he now fills ever since the institution was started, excepting about three and a half years, spent in visiting this country. He is assisted by four native teachers, all well fitted for their responsible work.

The whole number who have regularly left the institution is two hundred and sixty-one. Of these, one hundred and seventy-five have been employed in the mission, and one hundred and twenty-two were thus employed at the end of 1863. Some are in the service of other missions; some are in the employment of the government; and a few are overseers on coffee plantations in Ceylon. It is pleasant to know that some of these, at least, are not insensible of their obligations to the mission, nor indifferent in regard to its welfare. One recently sent a donation, amounting to one hundred dollars; and smaller sums have been given, not unfrequently, by others.

DISPENSARY.

A dispensary has been connected with the mission from its earlier stages. In the absence of a physician, it has been under the superintendence of a missionary, assisted by a competent native. Many have resorted to it almost daily, the number amounting, generally, to two or three thousand a year, embracing people of all classes and all religions known in the district. To all who have thus come, the truths of the gospel have been proclaimed, often under circumstances peculiarly favorable, and many have heard repeatedly. May it be found in the last day, that those truths have been made "the power of God unto salvation," to great numbers.

LITERARY LABORS.

Though there has never been a printing establishment in the mission, considerable labor connected with the press has been performed. One member of the mission was for several years associated with men selected from four or five other missions, in revising the Tamil New Testament; a work which required much time and careful study. The revision was completed in 1863.

The same missionary translated and prepared for the press a book of four hundred pages on theology, which has since been used as a text book in the seminary. One of the teachers in the seminary translated the abridgment of Wayland's Moral Science, another produced a small book, in Tamil, on the Life of Luther, and another a book entitled A Description of Madura. These three works were published by the "Christian Vernacular Education Society."

In 1853 the mission published a book of three hundred and sixty-two pages, containing a collection of Tamil hymns in English metre, a selection of chants, and a selection of "Sacred Lyrics, or Religious Odes, in Tamil Metre." The selections were made and the book prepared for the press by a member of the mission. The same person afterward made another collection of lyrics, forming a book of four hundred and seventy-five pages, which was published by the society mentioned above.

In 1854 the mission commenced publishing a Quarterly, in the Tamil language, under the supervision of the missionary just referred to, undertaken chiefly to furnish native assistants and other Christians with the means of mental improvement. This was continued four or five years, and translations of several useful works on science, church history, &c., were published in it, besides much original matter. Two or three other small books, and a few tracts, prepared by members of the mission, have also been published.

PREACHING.

Though great reliance was placed upon schools in the first years of the mission, preaching and the distribution of tracts were not neglected. Mr. Poor, who had a good knowledge of the Tamil language before going to Madura, was accustomed to preach daily, in school-houses and other places in

Madura city. Others began to preach in the vernacular as soon as they were able; but on account of the labors demanded by the numerous schools, the work of preaching at that time must have been confined, in great measure, to the villages in which the schools were located, and other villages in the immediate vicinity of the mission houses. As the schools began to diminish, tours for preaching in the more distant villages became more frequent. " Village congregations " sprung up, presenting additional inducements for laborers in the villages. It has long been the custom of most missionaries not only to preach, when at home, in the streets and lanes of the villages near, but to make frequent tours for carrying the gospel to villages more remote. Much labor of this kind is also done by native assistants.

The work of preaching has been constantly increasing for several years past. Excepting one or two, necessarily employed in other labors, the great work of all the members of the mission — the work in which they spend parts of almost every day — is oral preaching in the language of the people.

ITINERATING.

The subject of extending the gospel message to the more remote and destitute parts of the district has attracted special attention during the last three or four years. After careful deliberation, the conclusion was reached, that not only are additional men needed to be engaged exclusively in itinerant labors, but that those already on the ground should give still more prominence to this kind of work; and arrangements have been made for the regular and systematic performance of such labors in different parts of the district.

The following is from the report of the mission for 1863 : " A plan of itinerant labors was drawn up, embracing all the missionaries, so far as their circumstances would admit of their engaging in the work. Two missionaries, and as many catechists as they saw fit to employ, were associated together. The tents were first pitched June 1, and labor was continued till August 21, when the sickness of one and the medical duties of another caused a cessation of the work; and the rains coming on prevented its renewal by others who had arranged to take it up. * * * The gospel has been preached in three hundred and thirty-six villages and hamlets, to audiences which, in the aggregate, have amounted to twenty thousand persons; and a large number of tracts and Scripture portions have been left behind, to continue the work begun. This has been done in a region where there had been before little or no preaching of the truth."

The work of this kind done in 1864 was much more than that of the previous year, and it was commenced again in January of the present year, (1865.)

DISTRIBUTION OF TRACTS.

The distribution of tracts and parts of the Bible has been practiced from the first. They have been given to persons calling for them at the mission houses, and to those met in the highways; have been carried on preaching tours, and to fares and festivals, both by missionaries and native helpers, and distributed in great numbers, care being always taken to give only to those having the ability and expressing a wish to read them. The practice of *selling* has been introduced, to some extent, within a few years. This is important, both from the fact that a person paying even a small price for a book, will be the more likely to value it, and from the tendency of the practice to form the habit among the people of depending upon themselves, rather than expecting that everything will be done for them.

VILLAGE CONGREGATIONS.

A "village congregation" is one composed of several persons in a village, or in two or more adjacent villages, who have embraced Christianity, and are watched over and instructed by a catechist or teacher in the employment of the mission. Such congregations are always under the general superintendence of a missionary. When the head of a family belongs to a congregation, most or all of its members usually belong to it also. The first congregation of this kind was formed in the mission in 1843, in a village seventy-five miles south of Din-digul, where a man of influence had long been regarded as a Christian, and thir-teen families, embracing sixty or seventy individuals, had requested Christian instruction. Many such congregations had before this sprung up in one or two of the neighboring missions. In 1846 the number of congregations in the Madura mission had increased to forty, and in 1850 there were seventy-one, containing twenty-four hundred and seventy-one people. Five years later the number of congregations was one hundred and twenty, and of the people connected with them, five thousand and ninety-one. At the end of 1863 there were one hundred and fifty-two congregations, which contained sixty-three hundred and ninety-one people, representing more than twenty different castes, and living in more than two hundred villages and hamlets. Most of the people were originally heathen, but a large number were Roman Catholics. Persons proposing to form a new congregation, or to unite with one already existing, have ever been accustomed to profess a renunciation of their former religion, and to promise to observe the Sabbath, attend meetings for divine worship, and study the Word of God. As a general thing, a catechist or schoolmaster has been placed in each congregation, to instruct its members and conduct meetings. The larger and more important congregations have often had the services of both a catechist and schoolmaster. A catechist has sometimes had charge of more than one congregation, and in many instances the same man has performed the duties of both catechist and schoolmaster. A large majority of the catechists now in the mission have charge of village congregations, though it is made the duty of each to labor as circumstances will permit, to make known the gospel to the heathen. Most of the church members are mem-bers of village congregations. Most of the churches — all indeed but one — now under the care of native pastors, had their origin in such congregations.

The increase in this department has for a few years been less rapid in respect to numbers than formerly. For this there are several reasons. In the earlier stages of the work, the people often had mistaken ideas as to the advantages to be derived from embracing Christianity, and the missionaries were more liable than now to misunderstand the motives by which people were led to seek Christian instruction. Many made application from the impression that the relation into which they would thus be brought to the missionary, would tend to free them from oppression, or assist them in some case of litigation in which they were interested. Some, too, in the hope of being employed as teachers, prevailed upon others to join them in their application. But the people have learned that the missionary has the ability to do very little to shield them from injustice and oppression, and that the great object of his appearance among them is to promote their spiritual rather than their secular interests. They have learned, too, that no one can hope for employment until he has proved himself worthy.

Again, members of these congregations are now required to do much more for themselves than formerly; and this has doubtless had an influence upon the rate of increase. At first they not only expected the mission to pay their catechists and teachers, but to build school-houses and churches for them, and keep them in repair. Now, all are required at least to assist in the erection of necessary buildings, and the whole expense of repairs is in many cases borne by the people. Those who enjoy the labors of a native pastor are required to assist in his support, and some contribute toward the support of their catechists.

But though the numerical increase is slower than formerly, there are some things decidedly favorable. A much larger proportion than formerly are influenced, in coming, by a knowledge of the gospel, and a conviction of its truth. A greater proportion, too, are men of intelligence and property, and belong to the middle or higher castes. Men who have counted the cost will be likely to stand firm in the time of difficulty, and ultimately to exert an influence.

It is the usual custom for missionaries having village congregations under their care, to visit them each month, or as often as other duties will allow, "confirming the souls of the disciples, and exhorting them to continue in the faith, and that we must through much tribulation enter into the kingdom of God." These visits, in connection with which many opportunities are generally enjoyed for addressing the heathen, though laborious, often serve greatly to strengthen the faith of the missionary and to refresh his spirit. None of his labors are more interesting, none more important.

NATIVE CHURCH.

In one of their late reports, the missionaries say, "It is one of the principles of the mission to organize local churches as soon as congregations have become firmly established, and persons of approved piety have so far increased in numbers and intelligence as to make such an organization possible and useful. It is, further, the aim of the mission to place such churches in the hands of native pastors, as rapidly as men judged suitable, according to the apostolic direction, can be found to take the office."

The first church organized in the mission was at Madura, in October, 1836. It contained nine members, who had all been members of churches in Ceylon, and had come to Madura to be employed as catechists and teachers. A church was formed at Dindigul in 1837, and at each of the other stations soon after they were occupied. But they were composed almost wholly of native assistants, and persons belonging to their families who came from Ceylon, Tanjore, and other places without the district. For several years a large majority of the church members were of this class. In September, 1839, a church was organized at Tirumangalam, and a native convert received to it on profession. In 1840 there were twelve additions to the four churches, making the whole number of members, exclusive of native helpers, fifteen, of whom all but one were males.

In February, 1841, a church was formed at Sivagunga, with twelve members, three of whom were admitted on profession of their faith. One was a teacher of a free school. The same year, three boys in the boarding school at Tirumangalam were admitted to the church, and five adults, all heads of families, were received at Dindigul. In 1844 forty-three were added to the different churches, on profession — a greater number than had been thus received during all the previous years. In 1845, all the churches but one received additions, the whole number admitted on profession being twenty-four.

THE ACTION ON CASTE.

Allusion was made, when speaking of the seminary, to action taken by the mission, in 1847, on the subject of caste. The nature of that action, in its application to native helpers and other church members, and also the reasons for it, are explained in the following quotation from a report of the mission on this subject. "At first it was deemed sufficient evidence that converts had renounced caste, when they were willing to come out from among their friends, join themselves with foreigners, attend church, sit down by the side of persons of a lower caste, go to the communion table and partake of bread from the same plate and wine from the same cup. But after a time Christians could do all this without losing their caste, or being at all reproached for it by the heathen. What was at first a test became no test at all. High caste Christians would do all this, and more, without the least hesitation, or a thought of renouncing their caste. They did this while in the social relations of life caste distinctions were scrupulously observed. Even Christians would sooner go hungry than eat food cooked by a person of lower caste. Another test was therefore necessary." It was on this account that the following resolutions were adopted in July, 1847, viz.: —

"That the mission regard caste as an essential part of Hindooism, and its full and practical renunciation, after proper instruction, as essential to satisfactory evidence of piety; and that renunciation of caste implies at least a readiness to eat, under proper circumstances, with Christians of any caste, and to treat them, in respect to hospitality and other acts of kindness, as if there had never been any distinctions of caste.

"That we consider it to be the duty of all those who are members of our churches, after receiving proper instruction, to give us some satisfactory test of their having forsaken the evil, before we can, thereafter, administer the sacrament to them.

"That we will not hereafter receive into our service, as catechist, any one who does not give evidence of having renounced caste."

A large number of church members, including many catechists, refused to comply with the wishes of the mission, and were suspended from the church. But with the exception of nearly all the catechists from abroad, who left the mission, most of the suspended members subsequently complied, and were restored.

CHURCHES IN VILLAGES — NATIVE PASTORS.

In 1849 a church was organized in Mankulam, a village twelve miles from Madura. This was the first church established away from a station centre.

In March, 1855, a church of eighteen members was formed in Mallankinaru, connected with the Tirumangalam station, and a native pastor ordained over it. Drs. Anderson and Thompson, then in India as a deputation from the Prudential Committee of the American Board of Commissioners for Foreign Missions, were present, and took part in the exercises. This was the first ordination of a native pastor, not only in Madura, but in any of the American missions among the Tamil people. Five churches were organized the same year, in villages of the Mandapasalie station, and nine the following year, in villages of the different stations. The number of churches now in the mission is twenty-nine, of which eighteen are in the villages, and eight under the care of native pastors.

In their report for 1863 the mission said, "All the churches work harmoniously with their pastors, and, with one or two exceptions, much to be regretted, the church members, as a body, are harmonious among themselves. While we see deficiencies and imperfections, as a general thing it may be said, that our native churches and pastors are our hope and our crown of rejoicing. The number of church members at the close of the year, under the care of the native pastorate, is three hundred and forty-three, or, on an average, forty-three members to a church."

The whole number received to the church on profession, from the commencement of the mission to the end of 1864, is sixteen hundred and twenty-six, nearly four fifths of whom have been received since the year 1850. In 1853 one hundred and twenty-two persons were thus added, in 1854 one hundred and thirty-five, in 1855 one hundred and forty-four, and in 1856 one hundred and seventy-one. This is the largest number ever added in a single year. About two hundred church members have died in the hope of salvation, and one hundred and one have been excommunicated. Some have left the district; and at the end of 1864 there were eleven hundred and seventy-three resident members in good standing.

Upwards of thirteen hundred children have been baptized, and more than five hundred Christian marriages have been solemnized.

NATIVE ASSISTANTS.

The first natives employed in the mission were graduates of the Batticotta Seminary in Ceylon. Others were introduced from Tanjore a little later, and a few from Tinnevelly. Most of these left the mission, as before stated, soon after its action on the subject of caste, in 1847, or before that time. A great majority of those now employed have been raised up within the limits of the mission. Some have pursued a regular course of study in the seminary, and others a partial course. Some, employed first as schoolmasters, having previously had few advantages for education, received private instruction, and became readers or catechists. Not a few of this class have, in late years, enjoyed the advantages of the seminary for one year.

Nine native pastors have been ordained, one of whom has been dismissed at his own request, that he might remove to Madras.

The following list comprises the whole number of natives employed at the close of 1863: Native pastors, eight; catechists, ninety-two; readers, whose duties are similar to those of catechists, seventeen; teachers in the seminary and female boarding school, seven; schoolmasters, fifty-two; schoolmistresses, nine. Total, one hundred and eighty-five.

In 1851 systematic arrangements were made by the mission for the improvement of the natives employed, which, with some modifications, have continued till the present time. According to this plan, the helpers are brought together from all the stations once a year, for a meeting of three or four days, attended by all the missionaries. A sermon is always preached by a missionary, and the Lord's supper administered; and considerable time is spent each day in devotional exercises. Essays are read by natives, and addresses delivered by both natives and missionaries, on subjects of practical interest, previously given out. The helpers are also examined upon subjects previously assigned them for investigation and study. Once a year a meeting is held for similar purposes, in three or four different localities, by the missionaries and native agents of stations adjacent to each other, while each missionary holds a monthly, and in some instances a weekly meeting with the helpers under his particular superintendence, during which some time is devoted to their instruction. These meetings require much expenditure of time and strength; but considering their influence upon the natives, the number of persons employed, and the importance of this agency, the labor could not be more wisely bestowed.

NATIVE CONTRIBUTIONS.

As the number of Christians increased, the duty of contributing to the support of the gospel was urged upon them. From an imperfect understanding of their duty, and the poverty of many, the amount given was for some time very small, and is not large now; but the increase has been such as to afford encouragement. The sums mentioned below do not include the amount expended by Christians, in labor and money, upon their church buildings and school-houses.

In 1844 the amount given was sixty rupees, (a rupee is about half a dollar.) In 1850 two hundred and twelve rupees were contributed, and in 1853 eight hundred and thirty-six rupees, eleven annas, and five pice. The amount given in 1860 was a fraction less than eleven hundred and twelve rupees, and in 1863 it was sixteen hundred and four rupees.

A part of the sum contributed in 1860 was intended as a "jubilee offering," toward which a former graduate of the seminary gave one hundred and twenty rupees, another thirty, and one man gave a cow.

In 1853 the "Madura Native Evangelical Society" was formed, the object

6

of which was, at first, to support catechists and teachers in the more destitute parts of the Madura district. Since the ordination of native pastors, the society has devoted its income to the assistance of churches in their support. It is virtually a Home Missionary Society, and is accomplishing great good; not so much, however, at present, from the amount of money raised, as from its influence in awakening among the people a disposition to contribute to the support of their own Christian institutions. The annual income of this society is included in the sums mentioned above.

A great increase in the spirit of benevolence was experienced in 1861. This was particularly manifest during the meeting held simultaneously with the annual meeting of the American Board. A meeting appointed for prayer, one morning, was continued nearly four hours. In the words of the mission report for that year, "Many rose, one after another, each speaking a few earnest words, and laying down his offering. The giving was frequently interrupted by prayers. Some gave jewelry, some articles of clothing, and some pledged cattle, sheep, or fowls." About three hundred and fifty dollars were given and pledged at this meeting, and at a meeting held a day or two later, the sum was raised to five hundred dollars. A similar spirit was afterward manifested in some of the villages.

REVIVALS OF RELIGION.

Revivals — using the word in the sense in which it is generally understood in America — have not been often witnessed in Madura; but seasons of unusual spiritual interest have been frequently enjoyed, especially in the seminary and female boarding school.

The week of prayer has been annually observed since it was first proposed by the missionaries of Lodiana. For several years, additions have been made yearly to most of the churches in the mission. It has more than once occurred, that almost all the students of the seminary at a given time were members of the church.

In 1860 an interesting work of grace was enjoyed at some of the stations in Tinnevelly, particularly at the station nearest to Madura. Early in 1861, marks of a similar work began to appear at Mallankinaru, a village of the Tirumangulam station, in our own mission. Several persons were deeply distressed, at times, on account of their sins. Divisions in the church were healed, and church members became more prayerful and active. These manifestations continued for several months, and in addition to the results just mentioned, eight or ten individuals were hopefully converted, and professed their faith in Christ by uniting with his church. A little later in the year, similar seasons were enjoyed in the seminary, in several of the congregations of the Kambam valley, and in a few other places.

Of the work in the seminary, the principal spoke as follows, in his report for that year: "During the early part of the year, the religious condition of the seminary was very unsatisfactory, and caused me much anxiety. A few seemed to desire a better state of things, and were praying that God would pour out his Spirit. The week of prayer in January had been observed, but with less apparent interest than the year before; and altogether the prospect of a blessing from on high was very dark. This state of things continued till within four days of the close of the term in March, when, on the evening of the Sabbath, the Lord was pleased to pour out his Spirit in a most remarkable manner. One of the smaller boys was brought to me, in deep distress on account of his sins, and in an hour from that time four fifths of the students, including many who were members of the church, were in great agony from a sense of their sinfulness. This state of feeling continued during the remaining days of the term ; some, from time to time, finding peace in an assurance of pardoning mercy, while others were cast down with a sense of their guilt and ingratitude to the Saviour. All ordinary study was necessarily suspended, and the time was spent in religious exercises and in imparting such instruction as was suited to their peculiar circumstances. Subsequent experience has left no room to doubt that the work was of the Lord."

The following table presents some of the more important statistics of the mission at the end of the year 1864 : —

STATIONS.	When commenced.	No. of Churches.	Members in good Standing.	Received by Profession from the first.	No. of Village Congregations.	Men in the Congregations.	Women.	Children.	Total.	Average Sabbath Attendance.
Madura, ...	1834	2	148	202	19	181	165	241	587	538
Dindigul, . . .	1836	2	77	167	12	144	107	200	451	331
Sivagunga, . . .	1837	1	15	80	2	12	15	26	53	28
Tirumangalam, . .	1837	2	138	154	15	265	225	309	799	490
Tirupuvanam, . .	1837	1	9	10	4	19	21	43	83	65
Pasumalie, . . .	1845	1	59	160	1	30	6	24	60	112
Periaculam,	1848	2	40	16	6	77	86	159	322	151
Mandapasalie, . .	1850	9	362	522	44	552	524	719	1795	959
Usulampatty, . .	1856	1	—	—	6	41	32	49	122	88
Battalagundu, . .	1856	1	104	73	10	98	110	176	384	174
Malur, ...	1856	1	25	21	8	49	64	116	229	118
Pulney, ...	1858	1	39	35	6	71	53	99	223	138
Mana Madura, . .	1858	1	11	—	2	14	12	17	43	35
Kambam, . . .	1862	6	146	186	19	335	346	542	1223	565
		31	1173	1626	154	1888	1766	2720	6374	3792

I may be permitted to close this sketch with the exhortation, "Finally, brethren, pray for us, that the word of the Lord may have free course and be glorified, even as it is with you."

SKETCH OF THE MADRAS MISSION.

———∞◦❀◦∞———

THE Madras mission was commenced in August, 1836, by Rev. Miron Winslow, who was joined, the following month, by Rev. John Scudder, M. D. Both Mr. Winslow and Dr. Scudder had been members of the Ceylon mission between sixteen and seventeen years.

Mr. Winslow visited America in 1855, and returned in 1858. He left again in August, 1864, on account of ill health, and died at Cape Town, South Africa, October 22, two days after reaching that place.

Dr. Scudder left for America in April, 1842, with the hope of improving his impaired health. He returned to India early in 1847, spent two years in 'the Madura mission, and resumed his labors in Madras in March, 1849. He left again for the Cape of Good Hope, on account of ill health, in August, 1854, and died the following January.

Mr. P. R. Hunt, who went out as printer, reached Madras in March, 1840, and is still a member of the mission.

Rev. Samuel Hutchings joined this mission, from Ceylon, in April, 1842, and left for America, on account of ill health, in October, 1843.

Rev. F. D. W. Ward was transferred to Madras from Madura early in 1843, and left for America in January, 1846.

Rev. H. M. Scudder became a member of this mission in September, 1844, and removed to Arcot in 1851.

Rev. J. W. Dulles arrived in Madras in March, 1849, but was constrained, by the state of his own health and that of Mrs. Dulles, to return to America in 1852.

Rev. J. N. Hurd labored in this mission from July, 1852, until 1858.

THE PRESS.

The mission was established "for the especial purpose of printing the Scriptures and religious tracts in the Tamil language." As a printing press could not at once be sent from this country, "the church mission press was bought, in 1838, and from time to time enlarged, until it reached a state of great efficiency for printing, type founding, and binding." The establishment has not been restricted, as was at first designed, to "printing the Scriptures and religious tracts in the Tamil language;" but, as is said in a recent report, it is now "principally occupied in printing and binding the Scriptures, school books, tracts, and other religious and educational works in Tamil, Telugu, and Hindustani."

A vast amount has been done in this line, though the printing and binding of books is by no means all that has been accomplished. From a report, pub-

(44)

lished by the mission in 1864, it appears that *four hundred and twenty millions* of pages have been printed, more than half of which were of the sacred Scriptures. For the purpose of making the press as far as possible self-supporting, job work, not inconsistent with its objects, has at times been received. One of the works published is the large Dictionary, upon which Dr. Winslow expended much of his time and strength for many years. After some delay, from want of funds, this work was completed in August, 1862. It is a Tamil and English Dictionary of the High and Low Tamil, having nine hundred and seventy-six quarto pages, with three columns on a page, and contains sixty-seven thousand words, or thirty thousand more than any similar work. It has been highly commended, both by the press and by individuals, and is of special value to missionaries among the Tamil people, to whom it was dedicated by the author. In a communication addressed to Dr. Winslow by the Madras Missionary Conference, just before he left India, they say, among other things, " We can not let this opportunity pass without acknowledging, also, the great debt of gratitude we, as Tamil missionaries, owe you, for the excellent and elaborate Dictionary of the Tamil Language which it has been one of the labors of your life to compile."

But the character and large number of books that have issued from the American mission press at Madras do not indicate the whole value of its services. It has made great improvement in the typography of the Tamil, and some other languages of Southern India. The committee of the Madras Auxiliary Bible Society, in a late report, spoke thus upon this point: "Your committee desire to bear testimony to the important services rendered by the American mission press to the cause of Bible circulation, in the improvement it has effected in the typography of the vernacular Scriptures — a result entirely attributable to the exertions of Mr. Hunt, its zealous and indefatigable superintendent."

A few years since, a valuable gold watch and chain were presented to Mr. Hunt, by native Christians and missionaries of different denominations, as an acknowledgment of the important work done by him in improving the printing of the Tamil language. In the accompanying address the following language was used : " Every person who feels an interest in Tamil literature, in the well-being of the Tamil people, or in the progress of Christian enlightenment and civilization in a heathen land, must entertain a deep sense of the benefits which have been conferred upon the native community of Southern India, by the elegant editions of Tamil classical and grammatical works which have proceeded from your press, and which may be said to have raised printing to a place among the fine arts ; and especially by your clear, correct, and beautiful editions of the Tamil Bible, — each edition excelling the previous one, — which have called forth the admiration and merited the gratitude of all native Christians."

OTHER LABORS.

While the Madras mission has done so much by means of the press, it has also done much more. During most of the time he lived in Madras, Dr. Winslow was an active member of a committee of the Madras Auxiliary Bible Society, whose duties were of high importance, and demanded much time and careful study. Mr. Hunt has for a long time been agent in financial matters, as Dr. Winslow previously was, for all the Tamil missions of the Board, transacting for them much important business. The assistance rendered to new missionaries on their arrival in that strange country, and to others when obliged to leave, has been of the greatest value. Many who are now, or have been missionaries in India and Ceylon, will ever remember, with sincere gratitude, aid received from these mission families at Madras.

The mission has also done not a little in the work of education among the natives. From ten to fifteen vernacular schools for boys and girls, and one or two exclusively for females, have been in operation most of the time. In addition to these, an English high school was supported for sixteen years, much of the expense being borne by English residents. This school was brought to a close in 1861, (on account of the war,) when Dr. Winslow made the following remarks respecting it: "It has just passed its fifteenth examination. There were two hundred pupils of all classes, including many Brahmins. The school has done good. Several, by its agency, have been turned from dumb idols to serve the living God, and large numbers have been fitted for usefulness, and prepared to take respectable positions. Several are teaching in connection with government, or in various private schools, and five or six are in mission service as catechists or preachers." A report, published in 1864, says of this and other schools, "There have been several hopeful conversions of pupils while at school, and of others after leaving; in some instances when they were far away from the place where they were taught. The converts from the English high school, and vernacular schools for boys and girls, can not be less than eighteen or twenty in all, and though this is a small number, it is a great reward for the efforts made."

The preaching of the gospel has held a prominent place in the operations of this mission. Almost the whole time of Dr. Scudder, while living in Madras, was given to preaching and the distribution of tracts and books, both in the city and the surrounding country. For some time, he and his son, Rev. H. M. Scudder, made this their daily business, preaching regularly morning and evening, in different places of concourse, in the streets of Madras, and in the neighborhood of the city. Mr. Hunt, also, in addition to his work in connection with the press, has labored much among the people, with native assistants, holding meetings regularly on the Sabbath and the evenings of other days, in several places in the vicinity of his residence. Dr. Winslow was accustomed to preach to a large audience every Sabbath morning, and to preach or conduct a Sabbath school in the afternoon. The English high school under his care was opened with reading the Scriptures and prayer each morning, and religious meetings were held during the week.

A native church was early established, and since its organization about one hundred and eighty persons have been admitted to it, and one hundred children have been baptized. In a late report, Dr. Winslow said, "All our baptized children, on coming to years of discretion, have cast in their lot with the people of God. None have turned back to heathenism."

PROGRESS OF MISSIONS IN INDIA.

The Annual Report of the (English) Church Missionary Society for 1862–3, at the close of its review of the missions of that Society in India, not including Ceylon, presents the following "general view of the progress and success of Protestant Christian missions" in that land : —

"Ten years ago, tables were published by the Rev. Dr. Mullens, a missionary in Calcutta, of the London Missionary Society, exhibiting the statistics of all the Protestant Missionary Societies in India. Similar returns have been published this year, thus exhibiting the progress of missions during the last ten years. The enemies of Protestant missions have lately attempted to discredit their success, by presenting a collection of the many partial disappointments and failures inseparable from every great conflict between good and evil. The Committee regard Dr. Mullens' published 'Statistical Tables of Missions' as an incontrovertible and sufficient answer to the alleged failure. These tables contain the name of every Protestant missionary in India, where he labors, and what is his work, with true Protestant fidelity and distinctness. Taking the statistics of the *three Presidencies of India*, we find, that besides hundreds of thousands of listeners to the gospel message, there were, ten years ago, ninety-four thousand one hundred and forty-five registered Christians, and that there are now one hundred and thirty-eight thousand five hundred and forty-three. The addition of forty-four thousand four hundred registered native Christians in ten years may seem to some sanguine friends a small visible result, amidst the millions of heathen and Mohammedans in India; but those who take their estimate from apostolic times, and from the Lord's parable comparing the kingdom of God to a mustard-seed cast into the ground, will thank God for this result, and take courage. They will perceive, moreover, from these tables, that if the gospel plant has not yet shot up so high as to attract the world's attention, it has, nevertheless, spread wide and struck deep ; for whereas, ten years ago, there were twenty-two Societies laboring to evangelize India, there are now thirty-one, and the witness for the truth has been, thus far, more widely spread. The work also has deepened. Whereas, ten years ago, the converts were mostly scattered listeners, and only three hundred and thirty-one congregations of native converts meeting together regularly for Christian worship could be counted, there are now one thousand one hundred and ninety ; and these congregations contribute annually, out of their slender means, between forty thousand and fifty thousand rupees — that is, between four thousand and five thousand pounds sterling — for the support of their native ministrations, and for the relief of their own poor : whereas there were only thirty natives ordained to the Christian ministry, there are now ninety-eight : whereas there were eighteen thousand four hundred and ten communicants, these have risen in ten years to thirty-one thousand two hundred and forty-nine. Here are sure and blessed marks of a deepening work.

"The proof of success does not, however, rest merely upon the reports and statistics furnished by missionaries. Men of the highest authority and position in India, who dwell among the people, and who are responsible for their social prosperity and for public order, frequently come forward to bear their public testimony to the beneficial influences of missionary labor upon the well-being of India. Such men testify, also, their high appreciation of missions, by their large pecuniary contributions to the cause.

" The Statistical Tables of Dr. Mullens show that about fifty thousand pounds sterling (two hundred and fifty thousand dollars) are actually contributed by Europeans in India to the different Missionary Societies carrying on their operations in that country. Let it be borne in mind, that these fifty thousand pounds sterling a year are contributed out of their official incomes, in the midst of their official labors, by men who are looking forward to their return to England to enjoy the fruits of their savings; and the fact of such an amount of contributions, under such circumstances, will appear to be equally honorable to the men, and decisive of the reality and hopefulness of the blessed work for which they make such sacrifices."

The *Friend of India* presented a synopsis of the information collected by Dr. Mullens, respecting missions in *India, Burmah,* and *Ceylon,* a part of which will be given here. The tables were recast " to obtain comparative results," and to present a view of the " progress in each Presidency and Province." The *progress,* however, it will be seen, is not brought to view in Burmah, as the statistics of missions there, in 1851, are not given.

	Foreign Missionaries		Native Missionaries and Catechists		Native Christians		Communicants		Native Contributions	Boys at School		Girls at School		Total at School	
	1851	1861	1851	1861	1851	1861	1851	1861	1861	1851	1861	1851	1861	1851	1861
Bengal	103	113	130	206	14,778	20,774	3,500	4,710	Rupees. 7,872	13,283	12,634	1,490	1,976	14,764	14,611
N.W. Provinces and Punjab,	66	119	40	129	2,032	5,201	678	1,488	8,398	5,632	10,940	417	1,508	6,069	12,538
Bombay	35	40	16	63	744	2,231	230	965	1,708	4,045	4,006	1,323	1,436	5,068	5,442
Madras.........	170	210	405	973	76,501	110,237	10,032	20,218	75,370	29,896	33,082	8,109	11,007	38,005	44,080
Burmah	—	22	—	454	—	50,706	—	18,470	87,504	—	4,802	—	1,006	—	5,808
Ceylon	60	87	98	144	18,046	15,273	3,281	3,859	37,150	11,022	10,047	2,950	8,980	13,972	14,036
	443	541	608	1959	112,191	213,182	18,410	49,688	218,002	64,480	75,511	14,298	21,063	78,778	96,574